Kristy Didn't Want A Relationship. She Wanted A Besotted Rich Old Man Who Would Indulge Her Every Whim.

Jack stilled. Wait a minute. What was he thinking?

Kristy didn't want a besotted, rich *old* man. She simply wanted a besotted rich man. She'd probably marry a young one just as quickly. In fact, she might prefer a young one.

And Jack was a rich young man—at least he was for now, so long as he could prevent his grandfather from marrying then inevitably divorcing this one. It was up to Jack to protect his family's honor, not to mention its fortune. He'd wed her and bed her and in all the romantic haze have her sign a prenup, so that when she tried to cash in, he'd be ready for her.

Of course, he'd have to work fast.

And he'd have to be good, because she did seem sort of genuine, and definitely gave as good as she got.

Dear Reader,

Christmas is one of my favorite times of the year. I love a good, old-fashioned holiday season with twinkling lights, skating and horse-drawn sleighs. I also love a mistaken identity, particularly when it results in romance.

When billionaire Jack Osland believes fashion designer Kristy Mahoney is a threat to his family and their corporation, he decides the best way to neutralize the threat is to marry her. It's a great plan. And with the fantasy of Vegas and the splendor of Christmastime in Manchester at his disposal, the opportunities to romance Kristy are endless.

Unfortunately, Kristy is not who she appears to be. And, with the holidays looming, Jack quickly finds himself with more wife than he'd counted on.

I hope you're enjoying your own Christmas season, and I wish you the very best in the New Year.

Merry Christmas!

Barbara

www.barbaradunlop.com

BARBARA DUNLOP

THE BILLIONAIRE WHO BOUGHT CHRISTMAS

Silhouette®

Desire

Published by Silhouette Books
America's Publisher of Contemporary Romance

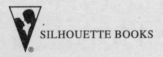 SILHOUETTE BOOKS

ISBN-13: 978-0-373-76836-3
ISBN-10:   0-373-76836-2

THE BILLIONAIRE WHO BOUGHT CHRISTMAS

Recent books by Barbara Dunlop

Silhouette Desire

Thunderbolt over Texas #1704
Marriage Terms #1741
The Billionaire's Bidding #1793
The Billionaire Who Bought Christmas #1836

BARBARA DUNLOP

writes romantic stories while curled up in a log cabin in Canada's far north, where bears outnumber people, and it snows six months of the year. Fortunately, she has a brawny husband and two teenage children to haul firewood and clear the driveway while she sips cocoa and muses about her upcoming chapters. Barbara loves to hear from readers. You can contact her through her Web site at www.barbaradunlop.com.

For Jane Graves, author extraordinaire.
You know the rest.

One

Jack Osland peered through the window of his Gulfstream jet plane as an indistinct figure emerged in the scattered snow falling on the tarmac at JFK.

"Did I even *mention* the word *kidnap?*" he asked his cousin Hunter who was sitting in the opposite seat.

"I can tell you're thinking about it," said Hunter, turning to improve his view, the white leather creaking beneath him.

"You're clairvoyant now?" asked Jack.

"I've known you since you were two years old."

"You were a baby when I was two."

Hunter shrugged. "You've got that telltale twitch in your temple."

"That just means I'm ticked off." Jack's attention went back to the woman who was striding through the frozen swirls of white. *Ticked off* was an understatement, and he was watching the reason walk toward him.

A slim five and a half feet, her face was obscured by a fur-trimmed hat and the enormous collar of her matching, cream-colored coat.

"Maybe she'll say no," Hunter offered, a hopeful lilt to his voice.

"And maybe pigs fly," Jack responded.

The woman wasn't about to say no. Nobody ever did. When Jack and Hunter's billionaire grandfather Cleveland Osland asked a gold digging, trophy babe to marry him, it was a done deal.

"Well it looks like dogs fly," said Hunter with a nod toward the future Mrs. Osland.

Jack blinked.

A flash of red pulled his gaze to her high-heeled boots. Sure enough. There, prancing along at her feet, was a tiny, plaid-coated fur ball.

As the implication registered, Jack shot Hunter a triumphant look. "Am I right, or am I right?"

"Her dog doesn't mean a thing."

"It means she's not turning around and going home."

"They only loaded one suitcase."

"You don't think Gramps's first wedding gift will be a platinum card?"

"Well, you *still* can't kidnap her," said Hunter.

"I'm not kidnapping her." Jack was desperate, but he wasn't a fool. He had no desire to give up a Malibu Beach penthouse for an eight-by-eight cell with a lumpy mattress, a leaky toilet and a roommate with a skull tattoo.

He didn't know how he was going to stop her. But, whatever his plan, he'd have to come up with it before the jet made it to L.A.

"What exactly did your mom say to you?" asked Hunter.

"She said that Gramps was at it again, and the latest one was hitching a ride with us. That's all I got, because she was boarding a flight to Paris, and we lost the connection. She's on the plane now."

"Could she have meant something else?"

Jack gave his cousin a deadpan stare. "No. She could not have meant something else. Gramps is getting remarried, and it's up to me to put a stop to it."

The future bride approached the aircraft, tipping her head to gaze at the fuselage. Jack caught a glimpse of straight, white teeth, burgundy lips, a smooth, flushed complexion and blue eyes that sparkled like jewels.

"Well, there's nothing wrong with Gramps's eyesight," muttered Hunter.

"I sure wish something would go wrong with his testosterone," Jack returned, giving the steward, Leonardo, a nod to open the cabin door.

"He doesn't sleep with them," said Hunter.

Jack stared at his cousin in disbelief.

"At least not until they're married. And then, well it sounded like sporadic attempts."

Jack was momentarily speechless. "You actually *asked* Moira and Gracie about their sex lives with Gramps?"

"Sure. Didn't you?"

"Of *course* not."

Hunter smirked. "You are such an easy mark. It was your mom who told me. I guess she asked them. She was worried about a possible pregnancy."

Jack wondered why his mother hadn't talked to him about her fears, instead of Hunter. Jack was her son, and the CEO of Osland International, the man whose job it was to protect the family interests.

Leonardo finished lowering the aircraft staircase, and the woman's quick footsteps echoed on metal stairs.

"You could try reasoning with her," Hunter suggested as they rose to their feet.

Jack snorted his disbelief.

But Hunter didn't give up. "Warn her that Gramps has done this before."

"She's a twentysomething trophy babe, dating an eighty-year-old man. You think there's a chance she'll be offended by his ethics?"

The woman in question rounded the corner in all her fur-trimmed, youth-dewy glory. The little dog barked once, but obeyed when she shushed it.

After a brief moment's hesitation, she smiled brightly at the two of them, leading with an outstretched, manicured hand. "Kristy Mahoney. I don't know if you heard, but I'm meeting with Cleveland and the Sierra Sanchez buying team on Monday. Cleveland said you wouldn't mind if I caught a ride?"

Her voice was as soft and husky as a lounge singer's. And she had an interesting flare of fashion—both for herself and the dog. In addition to the red plaid coat, the dog wore a collar that sparkled with rhinestones. After the single bark, it had stayed perfectly still, unblinking in her arms. It looked like a child's toy now, with wide glassy brown eyes and blow-dried fur.

Hunter was the first to step forward. "Hunter Osland. I'm one of Cleveland's grandsons. And of course we don't mind if you join us."

"A pleasure to meet you," she pulled off her white glove and gave his hand a graceful shake.

Then she turned to Jack and raised her finely sculpted eyebrows. Her face was porcelain-doll beautiful, with a tiny upturned nose, a delicate chin and wide-set, thick-lashed eyes.

"Jack Osland," he said, his voice unexpectedly gruff as he reached for her hand.

"Mr. Osland," she responded, closing her delicate fingers around his.

Jack was distracted by the feel of her cool skin, and her mesmerizing beauty. He barely heard Hunter's voice.

"Call us Jack and Hunter. Please."

She smiled into Jack's eyes, as if all was right with the world. As if she wasn't a shameless hussy hoping to get her hands on the family fortune. Quite the little actress this one.

"Jack, then," she said.

The sound of his name somehow sensitized his skin. Her vaguely tropical scent surrounded him, and her blue-green gaze seemed to bore directly into his brain. For a split second, he empathized with his grandfather. But he ruthlessly shook off the feeling. Unlike Cleveland, he wasn't falling for azure eyes, full lips and long legs on a woman who could barely string together a coherent sentence.

Not that Kristy appeared to be struggling with the English language. But her two predecessors sure had.

Gracie, Gramps's first bimbo, thought the bottom line was caused by poor-fitting panties. She had designed jewelry so ugly it had to be melted down and sold for scrap. Moira had insisted on her own perfume label. R & D on that little venture had set the family back about a million bucks.

With Kristy, apparently it was fashion. And since Cleveland was the major shareholder in Osland International, and since Osland International owned the Sierra Sanchez chain of women's fashion stores, she had a whole lot to gain from the impending union.

Jack, on the other hand, had a whole lot to lose. Reminding himself of that important fact helped him will his brainwaves back to normal.

"Welcome aboard, Kristy," he said.

His voice was even as he released her hand, but his brain was scrambling for a way to neutralize her. In less than five hours they'd be in L.A. That gave him five hours to figure out a way to save his family several million dollars.

This trip was the opportunity of a lifetime for Kristy Mahoney. She was trying to play it cool, hoping Jack and Hunter hadn't noticed the tremor in her voice and the slight shaking of her hands. It was a combination of nerves, adrenaline and way too much caffeine.

She'd been riding a high for a week, ever since she'd wrangled an invitation to a fashion-week after-party at Rockefeller Square and met L.A. clothing-store mogul Cleveland Osland. When he'd admired her self-designed gown, she was more than flattered. Then she'd been stunned when he'd asked to see her sketches and samples.

When he'd asked her to meet with his buying team in L.A., she'd begun pinching herself every hour on the hour, waiting for the illusion to vaporize. Any second now, she expected to wake up in her SoHo loft with Dee Dee curled up at her feet. She was sure she'd be tangled up in sweaty sheets, because this was better than any sex dream.

"Your coat, ma'am?" asked the steward.

Kristy switched Dee Dee from one arm to the other as she removed her hat and coat and her other glove. The man named Jack took in her straight black skirt and the snug red sweater, laced up at the front. Then he glanced disapprovingly at Dee Dee. Kristy felt her spine stiffen. Cleveland had claimed to be a dog fanatic, and Dee Dee hated to be left alone. Besides, she helped keep Kristy calm.

A year ago, Kristy had found the Pomeranian in a dank alley a few blocks from her loft. Cute little Dee Dee had popped out from behind a Dumpster, looking sweet, pathetic and small. Kristy hadn't had the heart to leave her out in a gathering November storm. Nor did she have the heart to let her stay at the animal shelter when no one claimed her.

Now she subconsciously squeezed Dee Dee as the steward hung her coat in the compact closet and Hunter gestured to one of the thick white leather seats.

"Please," he said.

"Thank you." Kristy sat down and crossed her legs, settling Dee Dee on her lap. The little dog's warm body helped chase away the butterflies in her abdomen.

"May I offer you a cocktail?" asked the steward as Jack took the seat opposite Kristy and Hunter sat down across the narrow aisle from Jack.

"Some fruit juice would be nice," said Kristy. It was nearly five o'clock, but she wanted to stay sharp. With the time-zone change gaining them three hours, they were scheduled to land in California at seven.

"I was about to open a bottle of ninety-three Cristal," Jack interjected. "We're celebrating the opening of a new Sierra Sanchez store in France."

Kristy hesitated. She didn't want to be rude…

"I could make you a Mimosa," offered the steward. "With fresh-squeezed orange juice?"

Kristy breathed a sigh of relief at the compromise. "That would be perfect. Thank you."

"Perfect," Jack echoed, obviously pleased as he leaned back in his seat.

He was wearing a Reese Gerhart suit, a Stolde shirt and a gray, diamond-patterned, Macklin Vanier tie. His studied, casual pose, along with the shock of dark hair that curled rakishly across his forehead, reminded her that she'd seen him mentioned in both *Business Week* and *GQ* in the past six months. Jack Osland—entrepreneur extraordinaire, heir apparent to Osland International, a man to see and to be seen with.

Beneath Dee Dee's sleeping body, Kristy surreptitiously pinched herself once more. Last year he'd made the list of the top twenty hottest male executives in America. Though, from her current vantage point, it could easily have been a list of one.

The jet engines whined, and the aircraft jerked to rolling, turning sharply to make its way to the runway. While they waited their turn in the lineup, the steward served the drinks— champagne for Jack and Hunter, and the mimosa for Kristy.

Jack immediately raised his glass. "To successful ventures."

Hunter coughed.

Kristy followed Jack's lead, toasting then taking a sip of the tart, effervescent concoction.

"So, tell us about your business, Kristy," said Jack, about three hours into the flight.

She placed her second mimosa on the burnished cherrywood

table between them. Then she took a deep breath, organizing her well-rehearsed pitch. "We're a fashion design company—"

"We?" asked Jack, cocking his head.

"Me," Kristy admitted, slightly rattled by the swift interruption. "It's a sole proprietorship."

Jack nodded.

When he remained silent, she picked up the thread of her pitch. "A fashion design company specializing in high-end ladies wear, specifically evening gown—"

"And what was your bottom line last quarter?"

Kristy hesitated. She'd hoped to gloss over her order volume and income, along with the modest size of her company. Although she'd been fighting for years to break into the New York fashion establishment, she'd yet to secure a retail contract, and her private sales were a whole lot less than stellar.

"I'm looking forward to the opportunities Cleveland can offer," she said, instead of answering directly.

"I'll bet you are," said Jack.

"Excuse my cousin," said Hunter. "He doesn't know when to stop talking business."

"I'm just asking—"

"Do you like basketball, Kristy?" asked Hunter.

Kristy turned to him and blinked. "Basketball?"

He nodded, taking a sip of his champagne.

"I…uh…don't know much about it."

"Cleveland loves basketball," Jack put in.

Kristy turned her attention back to Jack. "I'm afraid I don't watch sports."

"Hmm," Jack nodded sagely, his brow furrowing.

"Is that a problem?" She glanced at Hunter and then Jack, trying to read their expressions. Was it like corporate golf? Was Osland family business conducted at a basketball court?

"Would you recommend…" she paused. "I mean, should I learn something about basketball?"

"I would," said Jack.

"Jack," said Hunter.

"Well, I *would.*"

Kristy took a big swallow of her mimosa. Okay. Basketball. She sure wished she'd known about this earlier. She could have taken in a game, watched some ESPN or read a sports magazine.

Then she had an idea. "I don't suppose you two would share…"

Jack grinned. "Sure. He's a Lakers fan. And I wouldn't mention the Clippers if I was you."

Hunter jumped in. "I have tickets to the Lakers Sonics game on Friday, if you'd like—"

"Bud Reynolds is his favorite player," said Jack, shooting Hunter a glare. Then his more normal expression quickly returned as his attention shifted to Kristy. "The Budster is up for player of the year. He's ten for thirteen on threes from the straight away."

"And seventeen for thirty-five from downtown," said Hunter. "You should really join me at—"

"Kristy doesn't like basketball," said Jack.

She fought a moment of panic. "I never said I didn't—"

"She might change her mind," Hunter put in.

"I could learn," Kristy offered. If basketball truly was the golf game of the Osland corporate world, she was more than willing to give it a try.

Jack's mouth thinned as he spoke to Hunter. "Dating Kristy is not the answer."

Dating? She glanced from one man to the other. *Dating?* What had she missed?

"It's nothing but a basketball game," said Hunter.

"Drop it," said Jack.

Then a voice interrupted from the plane's intercom. "Mr. Osland?"

Jack pressed a button on his armrest. "Yes, Simon."

"Just to let you know, we're reading an indicator light up here."

A muscle in Jack's temple twitched, and everything inside Kristy went still.

"I'll be right up," he said.

"No need," Simon responded with a static crackle through the small speaker. "I'd like to have air traffic control divert us to Las Vegas to check it out."

Jack shot Hunter a glance.

Kristy tried to interpret his expression. Were they out of gas? Out of oil? Losing an engine?

He pushed the intercom button. "Your call, Simon."

"Roger that, sir." The intercom went silent, and Kristy's throat turned paper-dry.

Neither of the men spoke.

"An indicator light?" she rasped.

"I'm sure it's nothing to worry about," said Jack.

Kristy waited, expecting him to say more.

"That's *it?*" They were at thirty thousand feet, and something was wrong with the plane. She picked up her mimosa and took a healthy swallow.

"The jet is in perfect running order," said Hunter.

Her voice rose. "Except for the *indicator light.*"

Her thoughts flashed to her sister. Sinclair had begged her to postpone the trip until after the holidays. But Kristy hadn't wanted to risk losing Cleveland's interest. So she'd insisted on rushing to California.

If only she'd listened. If only dreams of fame and fortune hadn't clouded her brain.

Then she wouldn't be here. She'd be home and safe, instead of facing... She stared up at Jack. "Can you at least ask him what the light was indicating?"

"Kristy—"

She nodded to the intercom button. It was *her* life at stake, too. "Will you *ask* him?"

Jack heaved an exaggerated sigh. "Trust the pilot. He's a professional. And if it was serious, Simon wouldn't be chatting about contacting air traffic control. He'd be declaring an emergency and taking us down."

Kristy peered out her window at the last orange sun rays

in a darkening sky. She didn't see a fire, didn't hear any metal twisting, and the aircraft wasn't losing altitude or bouncing around. Then the steward appeared, looking calm and collected as he cleared away the drinks.

She supposed there would be a few more signs of panic if a fiery death was imminent.

"Relax," said Jack.

"It'll be fine," said Hunter.

But both men were on alert.

Then something banged on the airframe. The plane lurched sideways, and the steward nearly fell over.

"Buckle up," Jack commanded.

The man nodded, his face instantly pale. He slipped into the nearest seat and clipped on the belt.

There was relative silence for a few minutes. No more banging, and the plane stayed smooth, the engines purring normally.

"Ever been to Vegas?" Jack asked into the steady hum.

Kristy blinked at him.

"Ever been to Vegas, Kristy?"

She shook her head, stroking Dee Dee with a trembling hand. She wished now she'd left the little dog at home. At least then Dee Dee would be safe. Sinclair would have adopted her, Kristy was sure of that.

She blinked away a burning in her eyes. Sinclair. What if she never saw her sister again? Or her parents? What if her family was forced to watch the twisted, fiery wreckage of the jet on the evening news, knowing—

"Kristy?"

She glanced up to see Jack's expression soften with sympathy. "Everything's going to be just—"

The plane banged again, this time taking a sudden drop in altitude and leaving her stomach behind.

"Simon is the best in the business," Jack bravely carried on.

"That's reassuring, but it's the plane that's the problem," Kristy reminded him.

"It's just an indicator light."

"Well, it is indicating *something*."

Her fear morphed into anger. She knew it didn't make sense to be mad at Jack. It wasn't his fault they were all about to die. But he was the one arguing with her, and she couldn't seem to bring herself to think logically.

The intercom crackled to life. "Mr. Osland?"

Jack was quick to respond. "Yes, Simon?"

"It's the hydraulics on the right aileron. But we're compensating. And we're cleared to land. I don't want anybody back there to panic."

"We're not panicking," Jack responded.

"*I'm* panicking," Kristy hissed.

"He says he's compensating."

"What else is he going to say? That we should write our wills on a cocktail napkin?"

Hunter crossed to the seat beside Kristy. He belted himself in then took her hand in him. "If it was a serious danger, he'd be telling us to assume the crash position."

"Do we know the crash position?"

"Feet back, head down, hands behind your neck." Jack demonstrated.

Kristy tugged her hand from Hunter's and tried it, just in case, while the landing gear whined, and the wheels clunked into place.

Simon's voice came over the speaker once again. "Relax, everybody. Make sure your seat belts are tight. I'm not expecting anything but a slightly bumpy landing."

Kristy clasped Dee Dee to her chest, glancing out the window, trying desperately to quell the churning in her stomach.

She could see the outskirts of the city. The houses loomed large against the desert landscape. The strip rose up in the distance, glaringly brilliant and really quite beautiful from this angle. She'd give a lot to see the inside of a bright, clanking, smoky casino or even an Elvis chapel before she died.

"Kristy?"

"What?"

Jack reached for her hand across the table. "Look at me."

She glanced up as his warm palm closed over hers. She wondered vaguely how his hand could be warm at a time like this. Hers felt like ice.

"What the dog's name?" he asked softly.

"Dee Dee."

"Dee Dee's going to be okay," he said.

His eyes locked onto hers, and his deep voice rumbled through her body. "You're going to be okay. And I'm going to be okay. An hour from now, we'll all be laughing about this over wine and grilled lobster on the Strip."

Kristy didn't really believe him, but he seemed to be waiting for an answer. So she gave the barest of nods, and he squeezed her hand in response.

"Just keep looking at me, Kristy. I swear it'll be all right."

She held his gaze, and she started to feel hope.

The runway rushed up to meet them. The plane lurched to one side. Red emergency lights flashed in her peripheral vision. But for some ridiculous reason, Kristy kept her faith in Jack.

Two

As the Gulfstream finally coasted to a halt at the far end of the runway, Jack quickly rose from his seat. There was no reason for anyone to be hurt, but he wanted to make sure.

True to Simon's word, it had only been a bumpy landing, followed by a long stretch of deceleration. Even now, the emergency vehicles were struggling to catch up.

Still holding her hand, Jack went to Kristy first. "Okay?" he asked, peering into her eyes.

She gave him a series of swift nods, one hand stroking the little dog.

He smiled at her, let go of her hand and moved forward to where Leonardo was belted in. The man looked pale, but otherwise perfectly fine. Jack strode past the small closet and pulled open the flimsy cockpit door. "Simon?"

"All's well," Simon confirmed.

The copilot gave Jack a thumbs up.

There was a loud banging on the cabin door, and Jack quickly released the latch and lowered the staircase.

"Everybody okay?" shouted the fireman standing closest to the stairs. He was flanked by two others in their turnout gear. Behind the trio was a lights-flashing fire engine, an ambulance and two paramedics on the rain-spattered runway.

"We're all fine," said Jack as an airport security car pulled up, yellow lights adding to the show.

Simon appeared next to Jack's shoulder.

"A hydraulic problem," he told the emergency workers. "I'll meet you inside to fill out the paperwork."

"You need me for anything?" asked Jack.

Simon shook his head. "I'll take care of it. But you'll have a few hours to kill."

Jack nodded then turned to find Hunter and Leonardo both on their feet. Leonardo was helping Kristy into her coat, balancing the little dog in his arms while he tried to be of assistance in the narrow aisle.

"We might as well go inside," Jack said to them. "It'll take some time to do the incident report and look at repairs."

"Can I be of assistance?" asked Leonardo.

"Don't worry about us," said Jack. "Simon or I will call you when we know anything."

"Thanks," said Leonardo, handing the dog back to Kristy and giving it a pat on the head.

Jack gestured for Kristy to be first out of the aircraft, and one of the firemen came partway up the stairs to take her hand.

"I'm fine," she protested.

"It's slippery from the rain, ma'am. If you follow me to the car, security will take you to the terminal."

Jack shrugged into his overcoat and followed them down the stairs. Hunter was right behind him, and the three hitched a ride in the back seat of the sedan to the main terminal at McCarran International.

As the glass doors of the terminal glided open, he breathed a sigh of relief. Everyone was safe, and the plane was intact. But, as soon as those facts were neatly filed away, his pragmatic brain began calculating the silver lining. At the very least, he'd bought himself three or four hours. Because, despite his connection with Kristy during the emergency landing, his mission hadn't changed. And he now had some extra time to figure out how to stop her wedding to his grandfather.

The doors swooshed shut, and the noise and confusion of the main terminal engulfed them. They joined the crowd snaking its way past the luggage carousels and rental-car booths, and Jack fought an urge to put an arm around her shoulders and keep her close to his side. Ridiculous, he told himself. She'd had a bit of a scare, sure. But she was from New York City. This crowd certainly wasn't going to rattle her.

He raised his voice so that Hunter and Kristy would hear him over the din. "I say we head for Bellagio's." He couldn't see hanging around an airport for three or four hours. Not when Le Cirque was so close by.

"I'm going to grab a commercial flight," said Hunter, slowing down and stepping out of the main pedestrian stream. The escalator next to him stretched up to the departures level. "I've got a golf date with Milo and Harrison in the morning," he finished.

Jack glanced at Kristy, worried she might hop on a commercial plane, as well. But he quickly realized she wouldn't want to pay full price for a same-day ticket.

"I guess it's just you and me," he put in, before it occurred to her to call Cleveland and ask for his credit-card number.

Kristy glanced around the crowded terminal. "You go ahead. I can wait here."

Was she masochistic?

"My treat," he clarified, in case money was stopping her. He would have paid for her dinner in any case. It was his plane. She was his guest.

She started to back away. "I'm sure you have plenty to do without me hanging around."

"Like eat a steak and drink a martini?"

She smiled at that, and it was hard to imagine she was a gold-digging opportunist.

"Reports to read?" she asked. "Phone calls to return?"

It was nice of her to offer. Really it was. But didn't she know enough to shut up and take the free dinner? Besides, he had no intention of letting her out of his sight.

"I'm honestly only planning to eat," was his answer. And conspire against her, of course. But he didn't think it was necessary to divulge that bit of information.

She gave him a look that said she didn't believe him. "What about Dee Dee?"

"The hotel will take care of her. You won't be the first celebrity to show up with a pet."

"I'm not a celebrity."

"Yeah, but they won't know that. I'll get us a really long limo, and I guarantee the concierge will find a solution."

He could see she was still hesitating, so Jack brought out the big guns. "Do you really think my grandfather would ever forgive me if I abandoned you in an airport?"

Her eye twitched, and he knew he had her.

He knew he had her even before she opened her mouth.

"Okay," she finally said with a nod. "We don't want to upset your grandfather."

"That's right. We don't."

Hunter gestured to the up escalator with a jab of his thumb. "You two kids have fun. I'm off to find another ride."

Kristy gave Hunter a brilliant smile and moved gracefully toward him, her hand outstretched. "It was a pleasure to meet you."

Hunter reached for the hand, a goofy grin growing on his face. "Me, too. I'm sorry I have to leave you here."

"Don't be silly. You obviously have things to do. Me, I'm clear for the rest of the weekend."

"Really?"

Jack could see Hunter rethinking his golf game with Milo and Harrison.

"If you want to come along," Hunter said to Kristy. "We can probably catch something on United."

Jack wasn't about to let that happen. "Kristy's not interested in being stuffed in a last-minute back seat of a commuter jet."

"How do you know?" asked Hunter.

"Because she has a brain," said Jack, shifting in front of Kristy, squaring his shoulders and giving his cousin a crystal-clear *back off* glare. How was he supposed to save the family fortune if Kristy was off flirting with Hunter?

Hunter shrugged his capitulation. "Catch you next week, then."

"Yeah," Jack returned. "Next week."

With a wave, Hunter stepped onto the escalator.

Taking Kristy on a date. Of all the crazy, lame-ass plans. Did Hunter think he could dazzle her with his good looks and charm and make her forget all about Cleveland's billion-dollar offer?

Kristy didn't want a relationship. She wanted a sugar daddy. She wanted a besotted rich old man who would indulge her every whim.

Jack stilled.

Wait a minute.

What was he thinking?

Kristy didn't want a besotted, rich *old* man. She simply wanted a besotted rich man. She'd probably take a young one just as quickly. In fact, she might prefer a young one.

He stole a sidelong glance to where she was cooing at Dee Dee.

They were stuck together in Vegas. The land of glitz and glamour and fantasy. Where better to fall head over heels for a rich young man? Where better to have a rich young man fall head over heels for you?

And Jack was a rich young man—at least he was comparatively young. When you put him up against Cleveland.

Cleveland. What better way to make sure his family's reputation and fortune didn't take another hit, he'd get Kristy to marry him instead. And keep their money out of her hands.

Of course, he'd have to work fast.

Simon would lie for him about the jet repair, buy him tonight, maybe part of tomorrow. But eventually Kristy would get tired of waiting. She'd bite the bullet and buy a ticket on a commercial airline.

Until then, however…

He offered his arm and gave her a genuine smile. "Ever tried the tasting menu at Le Cirque?"

She shook her head, hesitating then taking his arm.

"Then you're in for a treat. Come on." He gently urged her forward. "Let's go find ourselves a really flashy limo."

Fortunately, since Jack ordered the tasting menu, Kristy didn't get a chance to look at it. If she had, she suspected the prices would have given her a heart attack. Everything about Le Cirque reeked of wealth and privilege.

The tables were covered in white linen, well-spaced, with comfortable, padded chairs. The service was impeccable, and the decor spectacular. Bold burgundy carpets covered the floor, while padded, striped chairs surrounded the tables and spotlights shone on recessed circus murals.

They started almost immediately with chilled cocktails, then she savored course after course of exotic delicacies complemented by fine merlots and chardonnays.

Afterward, Jack didn't even glance at the bill before handing over his platinum card.

His cell phone rang.

"I'm sorry," he said, reaching for his inside breast pocket.

Kristy shook her head. "Don't worry about me." She settled into the overstuffed chair, sighing as she gazed around the softly glowing room. The ceiling was draped with bright silk—yellow and orange and ivory fluttering like a tent dome around a central chandelier. It was dark outside, and the dancing lights of the fountains beyond the windows added to the intimacy of the restaurant.

"What time?" Jack asked into the phone.

Kristy took another sip from her wineglass, letting the tart, woodsy flavor ease over her tongue, as the room's ambiance seeped in and relaxed her.

"If that's the best you can do," he said, catching Kristy's gaze and giving her a smile that warmed her blood. "I understand. Okay."

He flipped the phone shut.

"Everything okay?" she asked, truly not caring for the moment. As long as nobody had gone bankrupt or died, she was going to enjoy her stolen evening with a handsome, intelligent and interesting man.

Things like this simply didn't happen to women like Kristy. Her last dinner out had been the bistro down the block. She and her date had split the bill. It hadn't been expensive. But watching him calculate the charges, add the tip and count out change had definitely taken any romance out of the evening.

"Simon's waiting for parts," said Jack.

Well, that didn't sound too dire. "What does that mean?"

"It means we're stuck here for the night."

Okay. That burst Kristy's little bubble. Cash-flow alert. She'd planned on finding a small family-style motel outside of L.A. Her travel budget didn't include Bellagio rates. Not even for one night.

"Don't worry about it," said Jack.

"About what?"

He reached for her hand, stroking his tapered fingers over her knuckles. "Whatever it is that made you frown. Don't worry about it."

"I have to worry about it."

"Says who?"

"My accountant and my credit card company."

He grinned. "Oh, that. Don't worry. I won't let you go bankrupt before morning."

She frowned at him. "Dinner was great, but you're not paying for my hotel room."

"Why not?"

"Because I have self-respect."

"You're my guest."

"I'm your fellow strandee."

"It was my plane."

"And you let me ride on it for free."

Jack sighed, and she could feel him regrouping.

He opened his mouth.

"No," she jumped in.

"You don't even know what I was going to say."

"Yes, I do."

"No, you don't." He got to his feet. "Come on. I'm going to show you something fun."

"You keep your platinum card right where it is."

He grinned, his eyes glowing in the candlelight. "Cross my heart."

She nodded. "Okay. That's better." She bunched her linen napkin on the table and rose with him. "So, what is it?"

He shook his head. "It's a surprise. It won't hurt a bit. But that's all I'm telling you."

"Will it be embarrassing?"

"Not in the least."

"Will I hate myself in the morning?"

His gray gaze went smoky, sizzling into hers for a split second, clenching her stomach, tripping her heartbeat. "I certainly hope not," he said.

"Jack—"

The sizzle evaporated. "Grab a sense of humor, Kristy. I'm not propositioning you"

She felt like a fool. "Sorry."

He held out his hand, the dare clear in his smirk.

She took a deep breath. Then she told herself to chill and curled her fingers into his palm.

His hand was strong, warm and dry, just the way she remembered. There was something about the texture of his skin, or maybe it was the way his fingers wrapped confidently around hers. It was the way it had been on the plane. She felt safe in his hands, as though he was in control of the planet, and all she needed to do was hang on for the ride.

It was probably a lingering emotion from the turmoil of the airplane landing, but it felt nice all the same.

They made their way across the patterned carpet of the casino. Machines flashed and chimed on all sides, while muted lighting showed yellow through draped fabric valences. Kristy tucked in behind Jack as he naturally cleared a path in front of him while he strode confidently through the crowd.

Above the buzz of conversation, a woman whooped in delight, and applause broke out around one of the craps tables.

The throng thinned, and they approached the casino cage where a neatly uniformed woman greeted Jack with a smile.

"Fifty thousand," said Jack, tossing his credit card on the counter.

Kristy turned to blink up at him like an owl. "That was a joke, right?"

He glanced down and gave her a wink and a mischievous grin.

"Seriously," she prompted.

But he didn't answer. Instead, he turned back to the clerk who handed him a receipt and a stack of bills.

Kristy focused on the money, trying to figure out if fifty thousand was casino lingo for some other amount. Maybe he'd meant fifty dollars or five hundred.

But those were thousand-dollar bills. And there were a lot of them. She'd never even seen a thousand-dollar bill.

Feeling panicky at the thought of him walking around with that much money, she pulled up on her toes and hissed in his ear. "This is nuts."

He leaned down to whisper back. "How so?"

"You can't blow all *that*." She was practically hyperventilating just looking at it.

He smirked. "I'm not blowing it. They'll give it back to me when I cash in the chips."

Like that was a reasonable answer. "Only if you *don't lose it.*"

He shook his head. "Have a little faith. I'm not going to lose it."

"You can't know that."

He tucked the bills into his inside pocket. "Sure I can."

She resisted an urge to sock him in the arm. "Do you have a gambling problem?" Was she an enabler in all this? Should she try to drag him out of the casino? Maybe call Hunter for help?

Jack grinned, turning to walk away from the cashier. "It's not a problem at all."

She moved up beside him. "Seriously, Jack. Should we leave?"

"I told you. This is going to be fun." He stopped in the middle of the casino and took a look around. "Okay, what are you up for?"

"A drink," she said, suddenly inspired. "We should go back to the lobby bar instead."

"They'll bring you free drinks at the table. Ever played roulette?"

He started to move again, and she scrambled to keep up. "No. Of course not. I don't gamble." Like she could afford to on her budget.

"Really?" he asked.

"Really."

"That's too bad." He stopped in front of a green numbered table and a shiny roulette wheel.

"Hop up," he said, putting the stack of bills down on the edge of the green felt.

She stared at the money, a sick feeling growing in the pit of her stomach. "No way."

He pulled out one of the high chairs. "Don't spoil the party."

"Jack, really—" Then she realized they were attracting attention from the dealer and the other players, so she lifted her heel to the crossbar and jumped up into the chair.

"That a girl," Jack murmured approvingly.

The dealer took his money and replaced it with a clear plastic tray of color-rimmed chips.

Jack took the seat next to her. "There you go. Now pick a number."

She glared at him.

"Care for a drink?" a female voice said from behind her.

"Glenlivet," said Jack. "One ice cube." He looked at Kristy. "A Cosmopolitan?" That was the drink she'd had before dinner.

She considered saying no. But two minutes ago she'd claimed to want a drink. She didn't want to look like a fool. So she nodded, and the woman jotted it down.

"Did you pick a number?" asked Jack.

"Twenty-seven," she said, giving up the fight with an exasperated sigh.

He nodded at the table. "Well, put some chips on it."

She picked up a single hundred-dollar chip and leaned over to the twenty-seven square.

"That's it?" he asked with obvious disappointment.

"You might be sure you're not going to lose," she said, as the dealer spun the wheel. "But I'm not."

"I never said you weren't going to lose."

"There you go."

He sat back in his seat. "What I said was, *I'm* not going to lose. And that's because I'm not going to play."

The wheel stopped on thirty, and the dealer cleared away her chip.

"See what you made me do?"

"Pick another one," he said, eyes dancing. "And this time live a little."

"Is this voyeurism for gambling addicts?"

He laughed at that. "I thought you said you wanted a room?"

"What does this have to do with getting a room?"

"You'll see."

"And it was *you* who wanted a room. I'm happy to wait at the airport with Dee Dee."

"All night?"

To save several hundred dollars? "Yes."

The dealer tossed in the small white ball.

Jack nodded to the wheel. "You missed that one."

She swiveled the chair to the side. "Can we leave now?"

"We've got drinks coming."

The ball stopped, and a sequin-covered woman next to Kristy gave a cry of joy.

"Play a number," said Jack.

"You're insane."

He lifted a stack of chips and placed them in her palm. "If you want to play it safe, take red or evens. Or, see that? If you put it on the line, you can cover two numbers."

Kristy squinted at another man's stack of chips sitting on the line halfway between two numbers. "Really?"

"Swear to God."

Kristy had to admit, that seemed like a pretty good deal. She put a stack on the line between seventeen and twenty. She refused to count the chips to see how much she was gambling.

Jack placed his arm across the back of her chair and leaned in. "Now don't let it rattle you if you lose. You're going to win some, and you're going to lose some. But we'll be fine in the end."

Kristy held her breath as she watched the white ball bounce around the wheel. It rattled to a stop on the seventeen.

She blinked, sure she must be hallucinating.

"You won," said Jack.

"I did?"

"You want to let it ride?"

She watched the dealer add a stack of chips to her bet. "Ha. What are the odds of it hitting seventeen twice in a row?"

"Exactly the same as the odds of it hitting any other number."

Kristy eyed him skeptically.

"Seriously," he said.

That couldn't be right. She reached out and moved her winnings to twenty-nine and thirty.

Then she reconsidered and cut the stack in half.

Jack sighed, leaning in to mumble in her ear. "We'll be here all night at this rate."

She ignored the warm puff of his breath on her skin. "I don't want to lose it all at once."

The dealer spun the wheel and tossed in the ball.

"There's plenty more where that came from," said Jack, tapping his finger on the plastic tray that held his chips.

"I can't believe you're so cavalier with your money."

"I can't believe you're so cautious with my money."

The ball bounced to a stop.

Kristy had lost.

"See?"

The waitress arrived with their drinks. Chatter ebbed and flowed around them as the sequined woman next to Kristy wriggled off her seat and slid to the floor.

A thirty-something man in a dark suit took her place.

He smiled a friendly greeting at Kristy. Jack reacted by leaning closer to her, closing the space between them.

She struggled not to grin at his posturing. They were about as far away as you could get from dating, yet some anthropological instinct had obviously kicked in.

"Make a bigger bet," said Jack, the fabric of his suit brushing against her bare forearm.

"Fine," she said, scooping a long round of chips and placing them on number four.

"Wow," he breathed, and she shot him a worried look.

But he was grinning. "Just messin' with you."

"You're a jerk. You know that?"

"Yeah," he chuckled.

She lost again.

"I don't like this game." It didn't matter that it wasn't her money. She was stressing out over losing it anyway.

"You're doing fine," he said.

"Can we do something else?"

"One more time."

She gave a hard sigh. "Fine."

Following the lead of the man sitting next to her, she placed a smaller stack of chips on the cross between four numbers. Then she took a bracing swallow of her cosmo.

The ball clattered around the wheel, settling on twelve, one of Kristy's numbers.

The dealer added a couple of chips to her stack.

"Low risk, low payoff," said Jack. He grabbed two stacks of chips and set them on number twenty-two. "Incidentally, that's also the way things work in real life."

"I know," said Kristy, watching in morbid fascination as the wheel spun around again.

"Do you?" he asked.

"Why do you think I'm going to L.A.?"

Astonishingly, with that much money riding, Jack turned away from the wheel to stare at her instead. "Is it?"

She nodded, not taking her gaze off the ball. "For the chance at a big payoff. I left my sister, my holiday shopping and my baking behind."

He kept his gaze glued to her profile. "Well, if this works out, you'll be able to do all the shopping you want."

"I suppose that's true." Then her eyes widened and her stomach clenched with the thrill. "You won!"

Jack stared at her a split second longer. Then he glanced at the roulette wheel. "I guess I did."

"Do it again," she urged. Clearly he understood the game better than she did.

His shoulders relaxed. "It's your turn."

"You're better."

He split his bet between number eighteen and the red zone. Then he pushed a stack of chips onto the line between eight and nine.

"Wow," said Kristy.

"What?"

"You must have a secret system."

He shook his head. "You pick numbers. It's completely random. Help me out here."

Scooting forward in her chair, Kristy gamely pushed a couple more stacks onto the board.

"Now we're talking," said Jack.

"That's a pretty rich bet," said the man next to her.

She felt Jack still.

Then the man glanced past her to Jack. His expression sobered, and he turned his attention to the table.

The ball hit the wheel.

Kristy doubled her money on two, and her bet also paid out on black. Several spins later, with her Cosmo glass empty and a new player at her elbow, they were up several thousand dollars. A man in a navy suit and a red tie approached them.

He introduced himself as the casino manager and asked if they'd care for another drink.

Kristy was pretty much done with alcohol. Besides, it was getting late. She hoped she'd won enough to pay for a hotel room because, now that she was tired, an airport waiting area didn't sound all that appealing.

To her surprise, the manager held out a key card to Jack. "Please accept the Ruby Suite with our compliments."

Jack gave Kristy a sparkling-eyed look. "Interested in a suite?"

"Two bedrooms?" she asked. It occurred to her that this could be a setup. Jack had been a perfect gentleman so far— maybe too much of a gentleman to be trusted.

He raised an eyebrow in the manager's direction.

Without missing a beat, the man pocketed the key and retrieved his cell phone.

"This is Raymond Jones. Can you bring me a key for the Diamond Suite?" He paused. "The roulette tables. Thank you."

He flipped the phone shut. "Two bedrooms," he said.

"And my dog?" Kristy asked.

"Not a problem," said Raymond.

"Then, thank you," she said with a nod and a smile. A free suite definitely solved her accommodation problem.

"Anything else we can do to be of service?" asked Raymond.

Jack glanced at Kristy. "I can't think of anything? Can you?"

Kristy shook her head.

Another man appeared at Raymond's elbow and provided a new room key.

Jack accepted it with a thank you, while Raymond gestured to the expanse of the casino. "Please. Enjoy the rest of the evening."

"We will," said Jack. "Thank you very much."

As Raymond and the other man walked away, Kristy turned to Jack. "So, did you pay him to do that?"

"Nope."

"Come on."

"I didn't have to pay him. The room's free."

"I don't get it."

"That's what happens when you bet big."

"They give you a free room?"

Jack placed his hand in the small of her back, gently steering her toward the cage.

There was something about that hand...

"If you're losing," he said. "They want you to stick around and keep doing it. And if you're winning, they want you to stick around long enough to lose it back to them."

"Is that what we're going to do?"

"Nope. Not unless you want to."

"I don't want to lose."

"Then I vote we cash out and enjoy our free room."

A free room with Jack.

Correction, a free suite with Jack. Two rooms, really.

She glanced up at his handsome face, and her stomach fluttered at the thought of such an intimate setting with such a sexy man.

Two bedrooms, she reminded herself.

Still. It was a hotel suite. And they were in Vegas. And she'd be a bald-faced liar if she didn't admit her mind was jumping to the possibilities.

Three

Kristy Mahoney was quite possibly the most perplexing person Jack had ever met. She admitted she was marrying his grandfather for money, yet he practically had to twist her arm to get her to gamble. They'd walked past designer fashions, fur coats and numerous jewelry displays in the hotel lobby, and she hadn't so much as sent a covetous look at the merchandise, never mind suggesting she needed a few things to tide her over until morning.

Any gold digger worth her salt should be demanding Cleveland send a new private jet by now or dressing herself to the nines on Jack's credit card. Instead, she was gazing around the luxury hotel suite in what appeared to be awe.

"It's huge," she muttered, her heels echoing on the marble floor of the foyer, Dee Dee's claws ticked along at her side as they stepped into the living room.

Jack shut the suite door behind them. "You were the one who insisted on two bedrooms."

She turned. "Did I foil your plans?"

He tensed for a split second before realizing she was referring to any plans he might have had to sleep with her. "I have no plans." At least not to make love with her. At least not tonight.

Though, if she'd agreed to one bedroom and hopped into a king-sized bed, he would have eagerly followed.

"Let me guess," she purred. "Other women generally fall for your 'come on up to my free hotel suite. Oh—'" she dramatically raised her hand to her lips, mimicking his voice "—look, there's only one great big bed.'"

He couldn't help but grin at her exaggeration. Yet, somehow her opinion pricked his pride. It seemed she felt he had no honor, and had to resort to trickery to attract women.

He found himself crossing the foyer to gaze down at her. "Kristy," he began in his own defense. "I'm a thirty-two-year-old man who works out five mornings a week and is in control of a billion-dollar conglomerate. What have I done to make you think I can't get women?"

She didn't miss a beat. "You're only thirty-two?"

God, she was spunky. "Ouch."

"And I thought it was Cleveland who was in charge of Osland International."

Ahhh. This one definitely had a better brain than the last two gold diggers.

"He's the major shareholder," said Jack. "I'm the CEO."

She shrugged. "I don't even know the difference."

Like heck she didn't.

"But, whatever," she continued. "I'm still not sleeping with you."

"Kristy, Kristy, Kristy." He didn't want her to sleep with him. Okay, yeah, he did. Obviously. Since she was stunningly sexy, and he did have a pulse. But what he really wanted was for her to fall for him.

Which meant he should probably stop yanking her chain.

But it was so much fun to tease her. And the woman could definitely give as good as she got.

"I'm sure you get women all the time," she conceded.

"Now you make me sound like a player."

"Are you?"

"No." He wasn't. He dated women occasionally. And he slept with women occasionally. But he was very discriminating. And he never led them on.

She moved to the middle of the living room, checking out the rest of the suite. "Got a girlfriend?"

"Not at the moment."

Her perfume left a trace in the air. It was nice. More than nice, actually. It wasn't fruity, yet it wasn't floral...

"Did she break up with you, or did you break up with her?"

Jack blinked. "Who?"

"Your last girlfriend."

"It wasn't a serious relationship."

Kristy turned back and nodded. "Ahhh."

"What's with the ahhhs?"

Was she accusing him of something?

"I know your type. Love 'em and leave 'em."

There was something in her eyes, not hurt exactly, but something. Had somebody left her? Was that why she was willing to settle for money instead of love?

Now he was curious, but he didn't want to bring up the subject of her love life. Because that would invariably lead to his grandfather, and Jack wanted her to forget all about Cleveland for tonight.

"I can hardly love you and leave you in forty-eight hours, can I?" he said instead.

"Forty-eight?"

Oops. "Twenty-four," Jack corrected himself. "I meant twenty-four."

"You scared me there for a minute."

He gave her his most congenial smile. "Wouldn't want to do that." Then he nodded to the glass balcony door and the view beyond. "How about a swim?"

She turned to follow his gaze.

He crossed the room to open the doors, implicitly bidding her to follow him onto the wide veranda. "Take a look down there."

She joined him to lean on the rail, between a pair of twin loungers at one end of the veranda and an umbrella table set up for four at the other.

He heard her suck in a breath as she gazed at the Mediterranean-style courtyard. The lighted pool was embraced by pillared fountains, terra-cotta tiles, tropical trees and sculpted shrubbery. It was peaceful and deserted this time of night, and the patterned pool bottom wavered through the mist rising from the heated water.

"It's almost midnight," Kristy whispered. "Are we allowed?"

He shrugged. "We're high-rollers in a complimentary suite. You think they'll stop us from taking a swim?"

"My swimsuit's still in the plane."

Had the woman never heard of shopping? Had she never heard of butler service? As if a tiny thing like a swimsuit would stop them. There was a phone on the table between the two loungers, so Jack picked it up and pressed zero.

The voice on the other end was prompt. "Yes, Mr. Osland?"

"Any chance we can get a couple of swimsuits up here?"

"Of course. I'll have the butler bring up a selection right away. The sizes?"

Jack covered the mouthpiece. "Size?" he asked Kristy.

Her eyes went a little wide. "Uh, four."

He nodded. "Women's four and men's thirty-two."

"Thank you, sir. Someone will be right up."

Jack replaced the receiver.

Kristy glanced at the phone. "Just like that?"

"Just like that," said Jack. Then he couldn't resist giving her an impish grin. "I'm hoping you get a bikini."

She eyed him up and down, a frown on her face that made him self-conscious. "I guess it's not quite the same for women."

"What do you mean?" Was it an insult?

She gave him an exaggerated shudder. "I mean, the thought of any man in Spandex."

He took a couple of steps toward her. "Did I mention I work out?"

"I'm sure you're perfectly gorgeous under that suit." Then she stilled as her own words obviously registered.

He was torn between making a joke and making a move. Deep down, he knew he shouldn't do either.

Still, he was suddenly aware of the way her eyes sparkled in the moonlight and her hair framed her face in gentle waves. That elusive perfume wafted through his senses once more. And everything inside him screamed at him to kiss her. Under normal circumstances, he'd definitely take the expression on her face as an invitation.

But these were not normal circumstances. He was on a mission. And he didn't dare scare her off.

He settled for brushing a wisp of her hair from her face. Her cheek was soft under his fingertips. Her lashes fluttered at the contact, and it was more than he could do to ignore the signal.

He subconsciously leaned forward, and she tipped her head to one side.

The knock on the door saved him.

Jack forced himself to pull away, his voice husky with burgeoning desire. "Our suits are here," he stated unnecessarily.

Kristy drew in a breath, and gave her head a quick shake. "Right."

He squeezed her hand gently, in silent acknowledgment of what they both knew had almost happened. Then he stepped into the suite and answered the door.

The butler handed him three women's and three men's suits on silk padded hangers. Jack tipped the man and sent him on his way.

Then he turned to find Kristy back inside the suite.

"Pick a bedroom," he invited, refusing to let himself look too deeply into her eyes as he handed her the women's suits.

She motioned to the closest door, the smaller of the two rooms. Again, Jack was surprised when her actions didn't fit his expectations. Either their almost-kiss had truly rattled her, or she didn't care about sleeping in the plush, four-poster bed in the main bedroom.

Either case was intriguing.

In the cool evening air, the pool water was chilly against Kristy's legs. A sultry breeze blew over her aqua, one-piece suit as she gradually made her way down the sloping stairs.

Jack on the other hand, executed a neat dive into the deep end, his shimmering form moving swiftly underwater toward her. He broke the surface, coming to his feet and raking back his dark hair with spread fingers.

"Feels good," he announced, looking slick and sexy in the diffuse garden lights.

"Feels cold," she responded, especially in comparison to the heat building inside her at she stared at his broad, bare chest.

He took a couple of steps forward. "Need help getting in?"

She reached out and gripped the handrail. "Don't you dare."

His grin was wide, showing straight, white teeth and bringing out a small dimple in his left cheek. His dark eyes sparkled. "It's easier if you do it fast."

She took a step down another stair. "I don't need your help, thank you very much."

She should have been worried about the cold water. And she was. But her mind also went immediately to Jack's slick, wet hands against her own bare skin, and her blood pressure took a jump.

She put her foot on the bottom of the pool, the water coming slightly past her waist.

He closed the distance between them. "My sister always screamed when I threw her in, but in the end she thanked me."

"I'm not your sister."

"You think I don't know that?" His gaze darkened as it dipped to take in her suit.

Her entire body clenched in reaction, reminding her all over again that he was sexy and smart and funny, and women around the world adored him. She definitely wasn't going to sleep with him. But that didn't mean she couldn't take advantage of the opportunity to flirt a little.

He shifted even closer in the waist-high water, and her mind waged a split-second war. Wrestling around in the pool at midnight was quite a ways past flirting. But then, he was only going to dunk her, not ravish her. Despite his joking innuendo, he had been a perfect gentleman all evening.

Still, they'd almost kissed on the balcony. And Kristy wasn't a complete fool. So, just before his fingertips brushed her skin, she did a surface dive, scissoring her feet, propelling her body away from him and into the deeper water.

"Chicken," he mocked as she came up for air.

"I prefer to take care of things myself," she responded, pushing her wet hair back from her face.

His forehead creased for a microsecond, and she thought he was about to say something. But then his expression smoothed out. "Where I like to help out as much as possible."

She kicked her legs to keep herself afloat. "You're such an altruist."

He gave a dramatic, self-effacing sigh. "This is true."

"*And* an egomaniac."

He swam closer. "Well, you're a tease."

"I am not." But she paused, reevaluating her behavior so far. "How do you mean?"

"Batting those come-dunk-me eyes, and then spoiling my fun."

She splashed at him. "Poor baby."

He grinned, then dove under.

Before she could react, his hand wrapped around her ankle. He tugged just hard enough to pull her below, then he instantly let her go, and she bobbed back up.

"Not fair," she sputtered, kicking over to where she could grab the edge.

He glided up beside her and rested his hand on the pool deck. "Who said anything about fair?"

He inched closer, his skin glistening with droplets of water, his hair nearly black in the shadow of the deck chairs. His eyes grew heavy with desire, and his voice vibrated her very core.

His thigh brushed hers, sending licks of energy across her skin. Her stomach contracted, and her lips went soft. She could feel an invisible pull compelling her forward.

"I've had some really bad ideas in my time…" she breathed.

He lifted her chin with his index finger. "And we're definitely going to talk about that someday."

She stared straight into his slate-gray eyes. Her chest went tight with emotion, and her body tingled with blatant sexual desire.

He tipped his head, light mist curling around his face as he leaned in. "But right now…"

Her body shifted forward, and she closed her eyes, savoring the sensation of his strong arms, his broad chest and his hard, hot thighs coming up against her own.

Their lips met.

His mouth was silky-soft, warm and mobile, with just the right combination of moisture and pressure.

She leaned in, bringing her breasts flush against him, wrapping her arms around his neck, letting him keep them both afloat in the deep water.

His hand splayed across her wet hair, holding her close, deepening the kiss. His hard thigh inched its way between hers and sensation burst through her body, coming out in a moan and a plea for more around their passionate kiss. She wanted to rip off her suit and rip off his suit and make wild wet love right here in the pool.

He broke off the kiss, moving to her neck, then outward, nudging the bathing suit strap out of the way to plant wet kisses on the tip of her shoulder.

She buried her face in the crook of his neck, inhaling deeply, flicking out her tongue to taste the salt of his skin. She threaded her fingers through his hair, tightening her arms, wanting to get closer, harder, tighter. Her legs went around his body, pulling him intimately between her thighs.

He slid his free hand up the tight suit, resting on her ribs, his thumb creeping along the underside of her breast.

She held her breath, as it circled higher and closer. When it rasped its way over her nipple, she groaned in his ear.

He swore in return.

Then he stilled, and slowly drew back, resting his forehead against hers.

"A little too public here," he breathed.

When her world settled back on its axis, she nodded in agreement, even as she tried to put some context around the experience. "That was…"

"Unexpected," he said.

She nodded again.

"Better make that surprising," he continued. Then he paused. "No. Better make that astounding."

He was right. On all counts.

"Tell you what," he began, his voice growing stronger.

She fought an urge to melt against him again. She didn't know what was happening here, but there was no denying she wanted more of it. They were both adults. And this was Vegas. If she got a vote, she'd vote they find someplace more private—say their hotel suite—to see where this all went.

"We'll dry off," he said.

She liked the plan so far.

"Then we'll go somewhere very public."

She started to nod, but then his words registered. Wait. The plan was off the rails already.

He drew back even farther, and the water sloshing gently against her felt cold again.

"And have ourselves a very decadent dessert."

Did *dessert* mean what she thought it meant?

She gazed into his eyes to find out.

"Don't look at me like that," he growled.

"Why?"

"Because I'm trying to be a gentleman here."

"I mean why *dessert* in a public place?"

He smoothed her wet hair back from her forehead, and gave her a melancholy smile. "Because I really meant dessert. Like I said, I'm trying to be a gentleman here. You said you didn't want to make love with me."

"But—"

He put his index finger over her lips. "Truly, Kristy. I don't want you to regret anything in the morning."

She wasn't going to regret anything in the morning. She'd said no lovemaking earlier, before she knew him, before she understood the power of the electricity and passion between them. They owed it to themselves, to the rest of their lives, maybe to the entire universe, to see where this was going.

"Would *you* regret it in the morning?" she asked.

He searched her face. "Not a chance in hell."

"Then—"

"Dessert," he said, with a small shake of his head. "And then our respective bedrooms."

A small part of her knew he was right. But a much bigger part of her railed against logic. She wanted to throw caution to the wind and drown in Jack's arms, even if it was only for one night.

She wasn't normally an impulsive person. But he brought out something latent and wild inside her, and she feared if she stopped it now she'd never get this chance again.

Maybe she'd regret it later, and maybe she wouldn't. "I don't see—"

"But I do see. Trust me on this one." His look was deadly sober. "Because I'm right."

Finally, she nodded, telling herself it would seem like a good decision in the morning.

* * *

At 7:00 a.m., with sunlight streaming through the window of the hotel bedroom, Jack wished he still thought tucking Kristy into her own bed had been the right decision.

He wasn't a man who normally questioned his actions. Once his decision was made, it was made. And for better or worse, he went forward from there. But at this particular moment, he was questioning. For one, he'd be in a lot less pain if he'd let last evening proceed to its natural conclusion. For another, she'd made no secret of wanting him.

And making love might have actually *helped* in his plan to romance her. He hadn't been dishonest about his feelings. Deliberately romancing her had been the furthest thing from his mind for most of the evening. He'd simply been enjoying himself with a bright, beautiful, funny woman.

Now, while the daytime traffic came to life on the city streets below—just past that eerie lull between five and seven while the gamblers and partygoers crawled into bed and the bakers and city workers ate breakfast—the right or wrong of his actions last night pounded uncharacteristically through his brain.

Following a private opening of the hotel boutique for slacks and T-shirts, he and Kristy had dried off and changed. Then they'd shared a sticky, sweet, chocolate volcano in the restaurant.

Watching her spoon the smooth, dark sauce into that pert mouth would have broken most mortal men. But not Jack. He'd kept his hands to himself, all the way through dessert and all the way back to the suite.

There he'd behaved like a monk, and he'd been inordinately proud of himself at the time. Because her flushed cheeks and smoky sapphire eyes had transmitted the kind of invitation that made his body beg for mercy.

And it was still begging for mercy.

And she was in the next room. Probably still sleeping, since the traffic noise and the whirr of a far-off vacuum in the hotel hallway were the only sounds in the silent suite.

He toyed with the idea of waking her up.

There was nothing stopping him from crawling in next to her in the warm bed and picking up right where they'd left off.

The worst she could say was no.

The best she could say was…

Instead, Jack reached for the telephone next to his bed. Seven in the morning with no sleep and a raging hard-on was not the best time to be making logical decisions. He punched in Simon's cell phone number.

"Captain Reece here," came Simon's staccato but sleep-edged voice.

"Sorry," said Jack, feeling a twinge of guilt for unnecessarily waking the man up.

"No problem. You ready to go?"

"Not yet."

"Okay." To his credit, Simon didn't ask Jack why the hell he was calling this early.

"Can you buy me another day?"

"In Vegas?"

"Yeah."

Simon stifled a yawn. "Sure. Shipment delay on the parts?"

"That'll do it."

"Done. Just keep me posted."

Jack chuckled. "But maybe not at 7:00 a.m.?"

Simon's voice relaxed. "That'd be nice. But I'm on call whenever you need me."

"Am I screwing up anybody else's schedule?" Jack asked.

Cleveland had exclusive use of one of the Osland company jets, while Jack was the primary user of the other. But Jack didn't need his jet every day, and other Osland executives frequently booked it when he was in L.A.

"Hunter called a charter company. We're covered."

"Great. Thanks for your patience, Simon."

"No worries. I'm fine. I'll grab some tickets for a show tonight."

"Have a good time." Jack hung up the phone, his hand resting on the receiver for a moment. He'd wondered if Kristy might enjoy a show. Cirque du Soleil was playing.

He rolled out of bed.

He took a cold shower and brewed himself a cup of coffee in the in-room machine. Then he picked up the phone to call his assistant.

"Hey, Jack," came Lisa's voice on her cell phone.

"Morning," he responded. "Didn't wake you, did I?"

"It's seven o'clock," she responded. Lisa was a morning person extraordinaire.

"Been jogging yet?"

"Just putting on my shoes."

"Well, I'm stuck in Vegas."

"Really? How'd that happen?"

"Jet trouble. Simon's having it repaired."

"You okay?"

"Fine."

"Why don't you grab a flight?"

"I've got a passenger." It wasn't really an answer, since commercial airlines generally had more than one seat available on their flights.

But Lisa was too polite to ask any questions. "You need anything from me?"

"Did we hear from Neil Roberts on the Perkins project?"

"Let's see." Something rustled in the background. "He says escrow will close on the factory Friday. The union agreements are almost finished—some sticking point on pension transferability. And the tooling for the robotics hit a snag in Bombay, but he's dealing with it next week."

Jack jotted a couple of notes on the hotel stationary. "Does he need me to call?"

"Didn't say so."

"Okay. I'll touch base with him on Monday. Anything else?"

"Harry's retirement in the New Year. If you want the engraving done on time, we have to get the order in now. Gold or platinum."

"You've seen them both. You decide."

"He'll want the gold."

Jack shrugged in the suite. He'd have gone with the platinum. But Lisa knew their Western Regional Controller better than he did. "Go ahead then."

"You sure?"

"You're the expert."

He could hear the grin in her voice. "It's about time you—"

"Have a good run."

"I will. Have fun in Vegas."

Jack grunted something noncommittal before he hung up the phone. He wasn't in Vegas to have fun.

His gaze wandered to Kristy's bedroom door. But having fun was certainly turning into a huge temptation.

He left his notes on the small desk and crossed the room to her door, knocking lightly.

"Hmmff?" came a muffled reply.

He eased the door open. "You waking up?"

She rolled onto her back, her blond hair fanning out across the white pillow, and her creamy shoulders peeking out above the ivory duvet while Dee Dee resettled herself on the foot of the bed. "I am now."

"Not a morning person?" His hand tightened on the doorknob, and he forced his feet to stay glued to the carpet while he let himself wonder if she was naked under the sheets.

"Not when I stay up half the night eating chocolate and ice cream."

Jack's gut clenched once more at the memory of how she'd dug into the chocolate volcano, her tongue curling around the spoon, rescuing a drop of chocolate sauce that had dabbed on her lower lip. He wondered for the thousandth time how he'd had the strength to send her off to her own bedroom.

He forced his thoughts back to the present. "I have good news and bad news."

She sat up, trapping the sheet under her arms, bringing it tight against what he was now sure were her naked breasts. "The good news first."

It took him an inordinately long time to find his voice. "We have tickets to Cirque du Soleil."

"I guess I don't have to guess the bad news." But she didn't look overly distressed at the thought of staying in Vegas.

Jack clenched his teeth, redoubling his effort to stay on this side of the room. "Simon's waiting on the parts shipment," he lied.

She nodded her acceptance of the explanation. "Any guesses as to when he'll get them?"

Jack mustered up a casual shrug, the words *Don't do it, Don't do it* turning into a mantra inside his head. He was proud of how normal his voice sounded. "Up in the air. We may have to do some more gambling to keep the room."

Kristy smiled at that, and the world shifted inside Jack. Her eyes turned the most incredible shades of blue. They sparkled like jewels when she was happy, then darkened to a smoky sky when she was aroused. He hadn't made her angry yet, but he'd bet anger had its own distinct shade.

For a split second he realized he was going to find out exactly how her anger looked come Monday. The thought clobbered him, until he shoved it aside.

She shifted to a more comfortable position on the bed, one delicate foot peeking out the side of the blanket. "You do know, don't you, that we could lose more gambling than the suite actually costs?"

He let his gaze rest on her perfect pink toes. "Law of averages says we won't."

"I thought the odds were on the side of the house."

"They are. But most people neither win nor lose big. And we'd have to lose pretty big to cover all this."

She glanced around. "True enough. If we're going to be stuck here, is there any chance we could get our suitcases from the plane?"

He forced his gaze from her bare foot and focused on the headboard behind her left ear, forcing himself to regroup and think logically about his plans. They could send for their suitcases, certainly. But that would undermine his efforts to make her feel like she was in a Cinderella fantasy. Clothes and jewelry were an important part of the package. She had to get completely caught up if he expected her to marry him by Sunday night.

"Don't you think it's more fun for me to take you shopping?" he asked.

She frowned. "I can't let you keep spending money on me."

He gave another shrug. "It's my fault you're stuck here."

She cocked her head to one side. "*You* broke the plane?"

"I own the plane."

She hesitated for a few seconds. "I guess you do, don't you?"

The question seemed rhetorical, so he didn't bother answering.

"This is all a bit surreal for me," she said.

Jack fought the urge to move farther into the room to reassure her. "Just go with it."

"Easy for you to say."

She was obviously worrying about Cleveland, and she'd think to call him soon if Jack didn't at least pretend to explore some alternatives.

He took a chance. "We could book commercial tickets, but that'll probably take just as long as waiting for Simon."

Then he held his breath and waited.

"I suppose," she ventured, clearly not convinced.

He tried to lighten the atmosphere. "We're marooned, Kristy. Think of it as being on a desert island."

She cocked her head, and he could tell his ploy was working. "A desert island that comes with a casino, chocolate volcanoes and Cirque du Soleil?"

"Hey, I had to pull a lot strings to get those tickets."

She gave a small, self-conscious smile. "Sorry. I'll stop complaining and lighten up."

"Yes. Do stop complaining. And do lighten up. We're marooned together until tomorrow, and there's nothing either of us can do about it."

She glanced around at the sumptuous furnishings and the rich curtains in the spacious bedroom. "I have to say, this is the best desert island ever."

Jack chuckled at that. "Come on, then. Let me show you the rest of it."

Four

Kristy sat up straight and peered past the Eldorado Tours sign to a mass of bright yellow, blue and red fabric that billowed out across the packed desert sand.

"What's that?" she asked, bracing her hands on the dashboard as Jack bounced the rented SUV into a dirt parking spot next to the porch of a small, graying building.

"It's a hot air balloon." He smiled, clearly pleased with himself as he shoved his sunglasses above his forehead.

She blinked at his profile. "You told me we were going to see the Grand Canyon."

"We are."

"But—"

He killed the engine and set the hand brake. "Did you think we'd ride down the cliffs on burros?"

She angled her body to face him. "I thought we'd drive up to the edge and take a look over." She'd never been to the Grand Canyon, but she imagined there were any number of lookouts along the main road.

"This is way better," said Jack. "We'll cruise down between the cliffs and get a close-up of the river."

Kristy's stomach dipped at the thought of skimming close to jagged rocks in something as fragile as a hot air balloon. "Is that safe?"

"It's safer than falling off a burro on a narrow trail."

She glanced back at the rapidly expanding balloon. "*That's* your benchmark for safety? Anything above falling off a burro?"

Chuckling, he opened the driver's door. "Don't be a wuss. You'll have a blast."

Taking a deep breath, Kristy reached for her own door handle, trying to remember if she'd ever heard reports of balloon fatalities in the Grand Canyon. She couldn't think of any, but that might simply mean the mathematical odds were catching up with them.

Jack rounded the hood and pulled on the top of her door, drawing it open the rest of the way.

"Have you ever ridden one?" she asked.

The roar of the balloon's gas burner echoed in the air as the huge balloon lifted from the ground, taking on a life of its own in a slight, desert breeze.

"A burro?"

She gave him an exasperated glare. "A hot air balloon."

"A couple of times."

"Really?"

"Sure."

She squinted at the bold yellow against the crackling blue sky. "How exactly do they steer?"

"They don't." He retrieved a small cooler from the back seat of the car. "You're pretty much at the whim of the wind."

"This is not reassuring, Jack."

He placed his free hand at the small of her back, urging her toward the gate. "The pilot's licensed."

"So? You just told me he can't steer."

"The Grand Canyon's a pretty big place. We're sure to happen across some of it. Where's your sense of adventure?"

"I left it on the jet."

His face suddenly tightened with concern. "Hey, you're not still freaked out from that, are you?"

She shook her head. Then she stopped. Now that he mentioned it, it was sort of unsettling to be going back up in the air again.

"Good." He took her at her word, increasing their pace. "This is going to be fantastic."

From the moment they lifted off the ground, Kristy had to admit, Jack was right.

The trip was better than fantastic. There was nothing quite like being above the ground, yet out in the open air. The balloon was slow and smooth. She was glad she'd worn a long-sleeved blouse, but with record high temperatures, the breeze was soft. Between the pilot's narrative and Jack's questions and jokes, she completely forgot to be frightened.

They soared the breadth of the canyon, dipping between layered cliffs of red, green and brown stone, nearly kissing the brittle, scrub-covered valley bottom, only to rise again and wend their way between spires of sculpted rock.

"With this wind, I can put you down at Narin Falls," said the pilot.

"Perfect," said Jack, giving Kristy's shoulders a squeeze. "Feel like a picnic?"

She nodded, relaxing back against him, content to be marooned and forget about the world for a while longer.

His arms wound briefly around her, his khaki-covered legs brushing against her new jeans, and the hard planes of his chest and stomach giving her a sense of security and certainty. She savored the feelings as long as she dared.

And then the balloon descended, following the steep drop of a cliff. It floated over a dusty plain until they came to a winding river with sprinkles of green lining either bank.

Then, in slow motion, the plain fell away. The river plummeted into a waterfall, burbling white and blue on its long drop to where it crashed into a turquoise pool surrounded by trees and shrubs and grass.

Kristy gasped at the sight.

"Hang on," said the pilot.

The balloon quickly lost altitude, the basket scraping along the sand, bumping to a stop several hundred feet from the oasis, the balloon canted over to one side.

Jack jumped out of the basket, steadying it with one hand, and all but lifting Kristy out with the other.

The pilot quickly handed him the cooler, then tossed a blanket over the side.

"We're clear," Jack called, his arm firmly around her waist, backing them both away.

The pilot poured on the heat, and the balloon reinflated.

"He's leaving," Kristy stated, trying to get her footing sorted out on the soft ground.

"He is," Jack agreed, keeping her clasped next to his side.

"How are we going to get out of here?" She'd seen the view from the air. They were miles and miles away from anything.

"He'll give the helicopter pilot our coordinates."

"We're getting picked up by helicopter?"

"Sure." Jack nodded, giving the pilot a final wave.

Kristy blinked up at him, the reality of the excursion suddenly hitting home. She was alone. Really, really alone with a man she'd only met yesterday.

She wasn't scared, exactly. What were the odds Jack had brought her by hot air balloon to a desert canyon to ravish or murder her? Plus, the balloon pilot was a witness. If Jack was a closet ax murderer, he'd be pretty stupid to let the only witness to the planned crime fly away.

Jack was a businessman, and an incredibly busy one at that. He was running an international conglomerate. She wondered, not for the first time, why he would take time out to entertain a virtual stranger. Taking her on an impromptu picnic didn't make any sense.

"I don't get it," she told him.

He glanced down at her. "What's to get? They'll send a helicopter. It's part of the tour."

"But—"

"Don't tell me we have to have the burro discussion again. Because I don't think they could even get burros in here. It's too far—"

"What I don't *get*—" she interrupted.

He snapped his mouth shut and gave her a chance to speak.

She took a breath. "Is why you're doing this."

"I'm doing this because I don't want to spend ten hours walking home after our picnic. We have tickets to Cirque du Soleil tonight, remember?"

The man was being deliberately obtuse.

"I mean all of it." He could easily have dumped her at the airport last night and gone about his business.

"All of what?"

Fine. She'd play along and spell it out for him. "Dinner. A balloon ride. A picnic?"

"Would you rather do something else?"

She pulled back from the arm that was still loosely around her waist. "You act like we're dating."

He let her go, fighting a grin. "Dating?"

"You know what I mean."

"Did I say we were dating?"

Okay, now she was embarrassed. "No, you didn't."

"Good. We're together on that at least."

She scowled at him. "You're wasting your time."

"No, I'm pretty sure I'm having a picnic."

"You should have left me at the airport."

"That would have been rude."

"I'm not your responsibility."

He glanced around. "Why are we discussing this now?"

"Because—" She paused, following his lead, giving a quick check on the desert around them. He made a good point. What was she hoping to accomplish by standing here arguing with him in the hot sun?

Answers, she supposed.

Like, what was he doing here? What was *she* doing here? She wasn't the kind of person to fall into adventures with rich, sexy, exciting men. Her life simply didn't work that way.

After a minute's silence, he lifted the blanket from the sand, gripping the cooler firmly in his other hand.

"We're here," he explained, "Because sightseeing is way more fun than hanging around an airport for two days. You know, you really have to lighten up, Kristy. You want to stand here and argue until we get sunstroke, or find some shade and break out the wine and sandwiches?"

At the mention of the food, Kristy realized she was starving. Her attention turned to the little cooler. "Sandwiches?"

He gave a sharp nod of approval and started for the oasis, tossing a final volley over his shoulder. "There. I knew you'd see things my way."

She scrambled to catch up, sand creeping into the crevices of her shoes. "I didn't see things your way."

"Sure you did. And that means I won the argument."

"There was no argument. And definitely no winner. We came to an amicable agreement involving shade, food and wine." She fell into step with him.

He slanted her a knowing grin. "You agreed to relax and enjoy the picnic."

"I did not."

He shrugged. "Okay."

"I merely accepted the fact that I'm trapped here with you for now."

"Poor baby."

She jabbed him with her elbow.

He hunched over to protect himself, but he was grinning. "Just make sure you don't have any fun. Otherwise, I'm the winner."

Kristy struggled not to laugh along with him. "Don't worry. I won't."

He glanced down. "You sure? 'Cause I think I see a smile in there."

She shook her head and pressed her lips together. "No, you don't."

"Liar."

She let herself grin, silently deciding to relax and take a breath. There really was nothing for her to worry about for the moment. Dee Dee was happy. She was having a great time with a concierge staffer named Randy and three other dogs staying at the hotel. A picnic beside a waterfall definitely beat an airport waiting room, even if it did mean Jack won the argument.

Maybe it didn't matter that today didn't reflect her real life. Fact was, it was happening to her. Against all odds and previous life experience, she was stranded in Vegas with a sexy billionaire who wanted to entertain her. She should enjoy it.

"What kind of wine?" she asked.

"Ha. Getting fussy are we?"

"No. I'm taking your advice and lightening up." On impulse, she covered his hand that held the cooler and gave it a squeeze. "This is incredibly nice of you, you know."

"I'm an incredibly nice guy."

"I'm serious."

"So am I."

She laughed, and then went silent as the ground turned from sand to sparse cacti, then to shrub brush and a few sparse pine trees. The roar of the waterfall intensified, and the spray cooled the air by several degrees. A brilliant glittering pool came into view amongst the rocks and willows.

"How did you know this was here?" she asked, glancing around in awe.

"The tour guy told me about it."

They came to a halt next to the pool, beside a small tangle of mesquite.

"We lucked out," said Jack. "Depending on the wind, we

could have ended up at Lone Pine, Condor Point or Dead Man's Gulch."

He set the cooler down on the grass to spread the blanket.

Kristy kicked off her shoes. "Dead Man's Gulch? Now I'm picturing alkali residue and bleached cow skulls."

"Not exactly romantic."

She did a double take. "Why would we want romantic?" Then she immediately wished she'd kept her mouth shut. They weren't dating. They'd been particularly clear on that point a few minutes ago. She should have let the comment pass.

He bent over the cooler, swinging open the lid. "I mean in the generic sense."

There was a generic sense to romantic?

Nope. She wasn't going to ask.

He retrieved a bottle of wine. "Oh, look," he announced. "The hotel packed Chateau Le Comte merlot. Now that's hardly generic."

He gestured for her to sit down on the blanket then took a seat beside her. The wind waved its way through the mesquite trees, while birds twittered from branch to branch. Jack rustled through the cooler, retrieving two long-stemmed glasses, a cork-screw and a plastic-covered platter of cheese and wafers. Making quick work of the cork, he poured them each a glass of the wine.

He smoothed back his dark hair and held his glass up for a toast. "To us," he said, his eyes going silver in the brilliant sunshine. "In the generic sense."

Everything inside Kristy relaxed. There was something so reassuring about his expression. It told her they were okay. They could go ahead and goof around, drink wine, see the sights, and it didn't have to lead anywhere.

She clinked her glass against his. "You know, this is about the strangest thing I've ever done."

He took a sip. "Yeah? Well, for me, it's not even close."

She tasted the fragrant wine. It was smooth and light, the flavor bursting in her mouth. Then she eyed him up. "You do realize that absolutely begs the question…"

He grinned. "It does, doesn't it?"

She nodded encouragingly.

He thought for a moment. "Let's see. If I had to choose, I'd say it was the fire."

That definitely got her attention. "You lit something on fire?"

"Hunter lit something on fire. I was only along for the ride."

Kristy took another sip of the merlot. "It was Hunter's fault. Of course."

"It was definitely Hunter's fault. He was upset. Still, if it wasn't for the gypsy and the elephants, we'd have been fine."

"You're making this up."

"I swear it's true. We were maybe fourteen and fifteen. We all went to the circus. Dad being Dad, and Gramps being Gramps, we got a special pass to go behind the scenes.

"Hunter decided to get his fortune told. But special pass or not, the wrinkled old gypsy made us pay twenty bucks. Trouble was, back then, we weren't as grounded in reality as we are—"

Kristy scoffed, practically choking on her wine.

"What?"

"Grounded? Your private jet has mechanical trouble, so a helicopter is picking us up after a bottle of Chateau Le Comte at the Grand Canyon. You call that grounded in reality?"

His eyes narrowed. "You want to hear the story or not?"

"Absolutely. Sorry."

"At least now I know I have to pay for the helicopter and the jet," Jack muttered.

"You've made amazing progress," she allowed.

"I have. Anyway. I told Hunter to keep his money. But he wouldn't listen. He paid her, and the gypsy gave us the standard someone-close-to-you-has-suffered-a-loss spiel."

Kristy had seen con artists at work before, testing basic questions until the subject engaged with one of them. "It could be an economic loss or a personal loss," she mused aloud, attempting to put the right quavering note in her voice. "Or maybe 'he has dark…no, light hair.'"

Jack jumped back in. "'He's old…no young…no maybe middle-aged…'"

"'Wait a minute,'" Kristy cried. "'He might be a she!'"

"You definitely get the drift," said Jack. "But Hunter was pretty impressed. The gypsy 'saw' that he'd cheated on a test and stolen his father's Jamaican rum, and he was convinced she could tell the future."

Kristy leaned back on her elbow and took another sip of her wine, trying to picture Jack and Hunter as spoiled teenagers.

"Which would have been fine," said Jack, gesturing with his glass. "Except she laid out the tarot cards and told Hunter he was about to meet his destiny. Tragically for Hunter, his destiny wasn't to become a rock star, it was to marry a young redheaded girl who would give him twin daughters."

Kristy started to laugh, not sure whether to believe Jack or not.

"You laugh now," he said. "But Hunter was convinced it was in the cards. So he decided he needed to steal her cards to change his destiny. We waited until she left the tent, then snuck back in. He paused for effect. "And that's when the elephants showed up."

"In her tent?"

He shot her a look of censure. "Of *course* not."

Kristy made a small circle in the air with her wineglass. "Well, of course there were no elephants in the tent. Because there isn't anything weird at all about this story."

"The elephants were outside on the grounds. But they were heading somewhere, and they shook the ground when they passed. And then one of them trumpeted, and Hunter nearly wet his pants."

"I'm sure he appreciates you telling this story."

Jack snickered. "He knocked over an oil lamp, caught the table cloth on fire and burnt up the tarot cards, the table and the tent."

"I wonder what *that* did to his destiny."

"Nothing. Six years later, he met a redheaded girl."

"No way."

Jack nodded.

"Did she have twins?"

"Nope. They broke up."

"That's not a very good ending."

"My uncle paid the gypsy thirty-five thousand dollars for the tent."

"Now *that's* a good ending."

Jack stretched out his legs and propped himself on his elbow. "She thought so, too."

Kristy followed his lead, straightening her blouse and jeans, then removing the plastic cover to snag a triangle of gouda. "What about you? Did the gypsy tell you your fortune?"

"That she did."

"What was it?"

He shook his head. "Uh-uh. Your turn to share."

"My life's boring compared to yours. Did your fortune come true?"

"Not so far."

"Well, what *was* it?"

He helped himself to a slice of havarti and a small, round cracker. "What do I get in return?"

"Twins?"

"Ha!" He nearly choked on the cracker.

"What do you want?"

He stared at her intently for a moment, while the waterfall roared, the breeze waved the mesquite trees, and the birds continued to twitter amidst the big, empty desert.

Kristy grew hot, then cold, and then very confused by her intense desire to kiss him.

"I'll trade you for a secret," he finally said.

She swallowed. "I don't have any secrets."

"Everybody has secrets."

"Not me."

Except maybe the fact that she wanted to kiss him. She hadn't murdered anyone or knocked over a bank. She occasionally didn't answer the phone when she knew it was her mother—especially if it was a Friday night, and she had a sappy movie on DVD and a pint of triple fudge chunk in the freezer.

But he wasn't getting that one. No way.

Jack watched her expression for a long moment. "Your first lover," he said.

Her throat went tight, and her voice came out as a squeak. "What?"

"Tell me about your first lover."

She drained her wineglass, stalling for time. "I don't think so."

"How old were you?"

"How old were *you?*"

"Seventeen."

"Really?" Despite herself, her curiosity was piqued, as was her imagination. She closed her eyes and gave her head a shake.

"How old were you?" he asked again, his voice husky against the birds and the breeze.

Kristy sighed. Fine. "Twenty."

He reached behind him for the wine bottle and topped up both of their glasses. "Ah. Late bloomer."

"No. An absolutely perfect bloomer."

Jack grinned at her expression. "Who was he?"

"A boy I met in college. It was in his dorm room and completely unmemorable. Now, are you destined to cross oceans? Father many children? Fly to the moon?"

"Buy a golf course."

He looked completely serious.

"What the heck kind of a fortune is that?" For *this* she'd told him about her first lover?

"The gypsy was a fake, Kristy."

"She was right about Hunter."

"The law of averages was right about Hunter. He's dated a whole lot of women of varying hair colors."

"But a golf course? That was all she told you?"

Jack hesitated. His eyes twitched, and he got a funny, faraway look in them. "No," he said. "She also told me I was going to marry a woman I didn't trust."

"I suppose that's better than having twins."

It was Jack's turn to drain his glass. "I suppose. You want to swim?"

"It's too cold. And we don't have suits."

He came to his feet, placing the empty glass on the top of the plastic cooler. "There's nobody around for miles."

She stood with him. "You're around."

"I won't look."

"I might." The thought came out her mouth before she could censor it.

"There it is," he said softly.

"What?"

"Your secret."

Five

They didn't swim. But Jack had accomplished his mission. Kristy was getting to know him, and she was still attracted to him. He was halfway home.

The helicopter had picked them up and ferried them back to the hotel. In the interest of time, Jack had made arrangements for the rental car to be picked up at the hot air balloon base. That gave them time for a shopping spree before dinner and Cirque du Soleil.

He picked Addias Comte, a shop just off the strip in an exclusive mall.

At first, Kristy resisted the idea of him buying her clothes. But he insisted and prevailed. And, after trying on a few outfits, she got into the spirit of the adventure.

"I'm not even coming out in this one," she called from behind the door of the spacious changing room.

"You have to come out," he countered, sitting up straight in the leather armchair in the richly appointed alcove at the back of Addias Comte.

Silence.

"Kristy?"

"It's…"

"What?"

"Fine." The door opened, and Kristy marched defiantly out in an emerald-green satin cocktail dress. It was cut low, revealing a wide swath of skin between her breasts, the V dipping almost to her navel. The waist was gathered in a wide belt, with a circular rhinestone buckle that would have done Liberace proud. The way the fabric was gathered around the buckle made her look like the back of a chair at a big hotel wedding. The skirt was split up the front, revealing almost as much thigh as tummy.

Jack loved it. But she sure wasn't going out in public like that.

"Next," he said.

"See?" she retorted, turning to flounce back into the changing room.

Next was a plain black pinstripe, very straight, buttoned up the front with a mandarin collar and a leather belt.

"You look like you're going to a funeral," he said.

"Something softer?"

"Something a whole lot softer."

She turned back into the room.

While she was changing, Jack asked the clerk to bring some jewelry, purses and a few pairs of shoes. Once she found the right dress, he fully intended to accessorize it.

The next one was basic black. It was strapless, with a small lace fringe along the neckline and a skirt that draped to mid-thigh. It was sheer and frothy, and he absolutely wanted her to wear it for him later. But it wasn't right for tonight.

"Too short," she said.

He nodded his agreement, but after she returned to the changing room, he instructed the clerk to wrap it for them when Kristy was done.

The next time Kristy came out, he knew they'd found the

right dress. It was a snug-fitting, shimmering gold sheath. Sleeveless, with a scooped neck and a tight skirt that came almost to her knees, it was topped with a three-quarter sleeve, cropped, black satin jacket.

"You'll need your hair up," he said. And she'd need a diamond choker, black stockings and some spike-heeled shoes.

"You like it?" she asked, glancing down at herself.

"It's the one."

She stared at him in obvious surprise. "But, I'm—"

"It's the one," he repeated.

Just then the sales clerk arrived with the jewelry. He picked up a diamond-and-yellow-gold necklace and earring set and walked over to her.

She watched him closely, looking both worried and excited.

"Try it with these." He unfastened the clip and motioned for her to turn around.

Her hand went to her throat, fingering the rich jewels. "Are they real?"

"Don't worry about it."

"Jack—"

"I said, don't worry about it." He managed to get the delicate clasp fastened.

She turned, and her cheeks were delightfully rosy. "I can't let you—"

"Put these on." He handed her the earrings.

Biting down on her lip, she slipped them onto her ears.

The sales clerk appeared. "Pumps or open toes?" she asked Kristy, holding up two pairs of shoes.

Kristy glanced at Jack.

He pointed to the pumps, and the sales clerk produced a pair of sheer black stockings to go with them.

He backed up to sit down on the chair again. "So now let's see the whole thing."

Kristy took a deep breath, but she went back into the change room without complaint.

"We're at the Bellagio," Jack said to the sales clerk. "Could you see if their salon will have time to do her hair tonight?"

"Certainly," the sales clerk answered. "Anything else?"

Jack glanced around. "The black dress. A negligee—something elegant, soft, with some lace. And maybe an evening purse?"

The woman smiled. "Right away."

While Kristy had her hair done, Jack bought himself a requisite suit at one of the hotel shops. Then he sat through an exquisitely torturous evening, hearing her laugh, watching her smile and seeing her move beneath that shimmery gold dress.

At the end of it all, he handed her the package with the negligee and all but ran into his own room. He didn't know what it was, but something inside told him to keep his hands off for tonight. He used every ounce of his willpower to stay in his own bedroom instead of begging her to make love with him.

But then Sunday dawned, and she was wearing jeans, and it was much safer around her in the daylight. They joked their way through a tour of the Hoover Dam, then had a late lunch on the deck of a Lake Mead marina and took a sunset boat tour. By late evening, they were just off the Strip, walking hand in hand, absorbing the energy of tourists and partiers.

Suddenly Kristy stopped dead, tugging on Jack's hand. "Oh, my God."

He quickly scanned the crowds around them, looking for trouble. "What?"

"Over there. A gypsy fortune-teller."

Jack shook his head, and reflexively backed away from the sign where she was pointing. "Oh, no."

"Oh, yes." She pulled hard on his hand, dragging him toward the gaudy, flashing storefront. "We need an update on your golf course. And I've never done this before."

"And you don't need to do it now." Three was definitely a crowd. He didn't need any distractions tonight. He was trying to think of a quiet spot back in the hotel, rehearsing over and over in his brain how he'd propose.

Not that he expected her to say no. Well, he supposed she *could* say no, since she already had Cleveland's offer on the table. And wouldn't that suck for Jack's ego?

He shook that thought right out of his head. All things being equal, Kristy should prefer him over his grandfather. After all, she seemed to like hanging out with him, and she got all his jokes.

Still, he was unaccountably nervous at the thought of popping the question.

Luminitsa the Gypsy—Your Future Revealed, proclaimed the glass door.

"Kristy," Jack protested, but he couldn't bring himself to physically stop her.

Bells jingled as she pushed opened the door.

He blinked to adjust to the low light.

The room had an orange glow, candles flickered on most horizontal surfaces, and the walls were covered with tapestries, bright-colored scarves and Celtic drawings. A woman with huge earrings, eyelashes a mile long and a silk kerchief wrapped around her head, emerged from behind a beaded curtain.

"Come in. Come in." She motioned with wrinkled, ring-bedecked hands to a small, round table.

Kristy eagerly slipped into one of the folding chairs, while Jack hoped humoring her in this wouldn't take too long.

He glanced at the walls until he saw the gypsy's price list. Then he handed the woman a fifty for the shortest reading she offered.

She waved her silver rings at him. "You, too. Sit, please."

Jack clunked into the other chair with a sigh.

"You are a skeptic," she said, arching one brightly painted eyelid.

"You could say that," he agreed.

Kristy nudged him with an elbow. "Ignore him," she said to the woman.

Luminitsa nodded, jangling her hoop earrings with the motion.

She held out her hands, dramatically waving them over the crystal ball positioned in the middle of the table. A spotlight shone on it from above. As she moved her hands in a series of sweeping motions, the spotlight became brighter, making the ball glow.

"I see water," said Luminitsa. "Maybe a beach. It could be the ocean."

"We're going to California," said Kristy.

Jack shot her a censorious look. The least she could do was make it slightly harder for the con artist.

The woman shook her head. "No."

"We're not?"

"Not today."

"Tomorrow," said Kristy.

"Maybe," said the woman. She eyed Jack, then Kristy, then turned her attention to the ball.

The spotlight had gradually turned yellow, then orange, making the ball seem to have a life of its own.

The gypsy suddenly sat back. "There was a plane crash."

Kristy shot Jack a look of astonishment.

He remained unimpressed. Everybody knew something about a plane crash somewhere.

"No. Not a crash," said the woman. "But something…"

Kristy opened her mouth, but Jack grabbed her knee and squeezed.

She turned to give him an impish grin.

"What about the future?" he asked. "Kristy's future." The sooner they got to that, the sooner this would be over.

Luminitsa screwed up her wrinkled face, peering intently into the ball that was now bright red.

She jumped up. "Oh."

"What?" asked Kristy.

Luminitsa glanced from one to the other, a sly smile forming on her face. "Congratulations."

Jack and Kristy's gazes met.

Kristy mouthed the word *twins,* and Jack rolled his eyes. He turned back to Luminitsa. "Congratulations on what?"

"On your wedding," she said.

Jack's entire body went still. Was there something in his eyes? Something about his posture?

"Wedding?" asked Kristy.

"Today's your wedding day."

"Which one of us?" asked Kristy.

"Both." She waggled her wrinkled finger back and forth between them.

Kristy's mouth dropped open. "To *each other?*"

Luminitsa nodded.

Jack grabbed Kristy by the hand. "That's it," he announced decisively, tugging her out of her chair and turning her to the exit.

The bells jangled again as they left.

"That was weird," said Kristy.

"We're in Vegas," he responded. "How many just-been-married or about-to-be-married couples do you suppose she sees every day?"

"I guess," said Kristy. "But that was weird."

For Jack, it wasn't so much weird as it was damned annoying. Luminitsa had just thrown a wrench in his carefully laid plans.

Kristy swayed to the music of Yellow Silk, the jazz band playing in the Windward Lounge, as she rested her head against Jack's broad chest. She was trying to pretend that she didn't care that these were their last few hours together. Simon had promised the plane would be ready by ten, and they'd be in L.A. an hour after that. She was wearing the lacy black party dress Jack had secretly purchased at Addias Comte, along with the diamond necklace and earring set, and she couldn't help feeling like Cinderella.

Too bad the clock was about to strike midnight.

She knew she should be happy. Tomorrow morning she'd

meet with Cleveland and the Sierra Sanchez buying team, and career-wise, she might just live happily ever after. Because if everything went her way, her life would turn on a dime. What she had dreamed of for years was suddenly within her grasp.

But melancholy overtook the joy in her heart. This was the end of such a beautiful fantasy.

The tempo slowed, and Jack gathered her close. She could feel the beat of his heart thudding rhythmically against her chest. His scent had become familiar. At some point, she'd started associating it with peace and safety, and she certainly felt that way now.

The fabric of the lacy black dress whispered against her legs. It clung to her breasts, nipped in at her waist, then flowed gently to midthigh. A Jacynthe Norman, from the winter collection in Paris, she knew it had to have cost Jack a fortune.

She'd have to leave it with him, along with the diamonds.

She wondered briefly if she'd ever see him again. If she was a supplier to the Osland Corporation, maybe they'd have a chance—

Then she stopped that thought in its tracks.

They'd spent a stolen weekend together. It was never going to be anything more than that. Their real lives were about as far apart as two people could get. He lived with the ultrarich in L.A. She lived with the struggling class in New York. Even if she did make a sale to Sierra Sanchez, they'd hardly be moving in the same social circles.

"You're so quiet," he murmured into her ear, his breath tickling her skin in a way that made her long for his lips to brush up against her. She itched for it. She ached for it.

"Just thinking," she said, splaying her hand over the taut muscles of his back.

"About?"

She tipped her head to look up at him. "Tomorrow."

He paused. "Really? I'm thinking about tonight."

"You worried about the plane?"

He shook his head, his eyes turning the color of thick smoke, as his hand slid up her ribcage, brushing purposefully against the side of her breast. "I'm not thinking quite that far in the future."

Her heart thudded in response to his caress. Her skin prickled with anticipation. And her body convulsed with longing.

She swallowed, hardly able to form the words. "We still have the suite."

He stared at her, but didn't say a word. Then his arm tightened firmly around her waist, and he turned them both toward the nightclub door.

Outside, the air was sultry warm, thunderclouds had gathered above the skyscrapers, holding the daytime heat. Their forked lightning strikes sparked like lasers in the haze, faint thunder echoing after. Halfway down the block, the first raindrops splattered on the warm concrete, and Kristy and Jack joined the other tourists who scattered for shelter.

Damp and laughing, they made it to the Bellagio lobby.

Jack turned to look at her, taking in the rain-spattered dress, smoothing her damp hair back from her face. "You are so beautiful."

Kristy inhaled. "So are you."

He glanced at his watch. "We've only got a couple of hours." Then he looked into her eyes again, voice bedroom-husky. "I can't believe we put this off so long."

"What were we thinking?"

He took her hand and started across the lobby. "I don't know."

But instead of heading for the main elevator block which provided the more direct line to their room, he took a circuitous route past the shops. She wondered if they needed something from a store. Condoms, maybe? It wasn't the height of romance, but she supposed practical was practical.

But they carried on past the Essentials store, around the courtyard pool area.

"Did you rent us a cabana?" she asked. The suite was fine. The suite was wonderful. And, really, the clock was ticking.

Jack shook his head. He slowed, turning to look at her as they passed the grand balcony. "I don't want this to end."

"The walk to our room?"

His mouth curved in an ironic grin. He squeezed her hand while shaking his head. "You and me."

She peered at his expression. "I don't understand."

He nodded to a spot in front of them, and she followed his gaze. The East Chapel.

"Marry me, Kristy."

She stopped dead. "Huh?"

He held her gaze with his own. "Did something ever seem completely right to you?"

"What?" Had he lost his mind? Yeah, they were having a fantastic weekend. And yeah, she couldn't wait to get back to the suite and tear off his clothes. But this wasn't 1952. They could make love without getting married.

"This feels right," he repeated. "I know it's right."

She took a step toward him. "Jack. The fortune-teller was a fraud."

"This has nothing to do with the fortune-teller."

"Then what does it have to do with?"

"You and me."

"You and me are about to make love."

"Yeah," he nodded. "Over and over again if I have my way."

Kristy glanced at her own watch. "Not unless you're a whole lot faster at it than I've fantasized."

He drew back. "You've fantasized?"

"Yeah," she admitted. "Haven't you?"

"Oh, yeah." His eyes went softer still. He blinked. "Marry me, Kristy."

"No."

A group of partiers rounded the corner, their drunken shouts and laughter intruding on the moment.

Jack whisked Kristy to a glass door, opening it to steer her onto a pillared patio overlooking the pools. He closed the door behind them.

"Listen to me," he said.

"Jack," she sighed, fighting hard to hold her emotional ground.

Truth was, making love to Jack over and over again for the rest of her life sounded really good right now. And there was a deceptive intimacy to huddling in the sheltered darkness while the storm rumbled and flashed in the sky. Raindrops battered the waxy leaves of the potted tropical plants, while a film of steam rose from the pool decks and fountains, obscuring the pot lights, giving the entire garden an eerie glow.

He moved in close, his whisper tortured and husky. "I can't lose this chance. I can't let you go."

She squinted. Was he serious? Did he really want to see her again? Romantically?

She'd hardly dared hope.

No. Scratch that. She *wouldn't* dare hope.

His fingertips brushed her cheek. "This is something, Kristy."

Her chest contracted. She had to agree with him there. This was definitely something.

"Have you ever—" he breathed. Then he closed his eyes for a second, as if gathering his thoughts. "Have you ever, in your entire life, ever felt this way?"

She slowly shook her head. There were no words to describe how she felt about Jack—the passion, the admiration, the deep-down soul connection.

"We can't let it go," he said.

"We don't have to let it go." They could see each other again. He could come to New York. Heck, he had an office there, and his own jet plane. He could drop by and see her whenever he was in town.

He ran his hands up and down her arms. "How many people do you suppose say that?"

"Say they'll get together again?"

He nodded. "Hundreds, maybe thousands. And how many of them ever do?"

She shrugged. Not many, she'd suspect, and that gave her a hollow feeling in the pit of her stomach.

"We leave this hotel, Kristy, and you know as well as I do that'll be it."

Would it? Would they really walk away from a connection this strong?

"You'll go back to New York. I'll go to L.A. We'll e-mail, maybe call. But pretty soon, our memories will fade. We'll decide it couldn't have been as great as we thought. We'll write each other off as a weekend fling."

She found her voice. "We *are* a weekend fling."

"We don't have to be." His hands met her upper arms, his voice going earnest. "We can be better than that. Let me make it so we… So *I* have to be better than that."

She knew he was talking crazy. People didn't get married to guarantee a second date. She opened her mouth to tell him so, but he put an index finger across her lips.

His gaze bore directly into hers. "I think I'm falling in love with you, Kristy."

Her entire body convulsed with a wash of emotions and hormones. Love? Could this possibly be love?

"Don't let me walk away from you, Kristy. Don't let me be the man I know I'll be."

She wanted to say yes. In every fiber of her being, she longed to complete the fantasy.

Love.

She rolled the idea around in her brain.

She didn't know anything about romantic love, but she'd sure never felt this way about any man before. And if this was as good as it got… Well, it was pretty darn good—talking, laughing, touching. All Jack, all day, every day, for ever and ever.

"Marry me," he groaned, his hand tunneling into her damp hair, cupping her head, drawing her forward. "Make me come back to you."

And then he kissed her. His hot lips possessing and devouring her own. Raw passion permeated every breath, as the wind swirled around them, tearing at their clothes, rattling the broad leaves. The staccato beat of the rain matched the frantic melding of their hearts.

She clung to his shoulders, tipping her head to deepen the kiss, her spine bending as she leaned back, baring her neck and chest and body to him. He peppered kisses on the exposed flesh, cupping his hand over her breast where her nipple had puckered beneath the thin, damp fabric. Sparks flew off in all directions, lighting her brain, making her feel as though absolute clarity was within her grasp.

The world fell away until there was nothing but Jack. Their differences didn't matter. Geography didn't matter. Fashion, business, money and power. None of it mattered. There weren't two of them anymore, only one. And the universe would have to settle around that reality.

She anchored her hands in his thick hair, drawing him back, staring into his passion-clouded eyes.

"Yes," she said. "Yes, yes and yes."

He sighed. Then he entwined his fingers with hers, straightening until he faced her. "You have made me unbelievably happy."

Kristy smiled at him, everything inside her going calm. They'd make it work. She knew with an absolute certainty that she could put her faith in Jack.

Hand in hand, they floated down the hallway to the hotel chapel.

There, Kristy was given a delicate bouquet of white roses. They signed a bunch of papers. Jack asked the organist to play "At Last," and he chose plain gold bands, whispering promises of diamonds in her future.

But Kristy didn't need diamonds. She didn't need designer clothes or corporate jets or a high-end penthouse. All she needed was Jack. And, as the chaplain asked her to repeat the age-old vows of faith and fidelity, she knew she was getting Jack forever.

* * *

Next to the big four-poster bed, with Kristy in his arms, Jack ignored the heated accusations of betrayal and deceit that pounded away at his brain. Instead, he peeled away her silk dress, revealing her creamy, pink-tipped breasts, and honestly told himself he was the luckiest man in the world.

"Beautiful," he murmured more to himself than to her. "So beautiful." Then he placed a soft kiss on one tip and then the other.

Kristy drew in a gasp of pleasure, her fingers curling into his hair.

"I love you," she gasped, and a knife twisted deep inside his heart.

"And I'm about to love you," he growled in return, hating that he had to fudge the phrase. She deserved better.

"For just as long as you'll let me," he finished.

Then he tugged her dress down to her ankles and gently pushed her back on the bed to stare at smooth stomach, her lacy black panties and the creamy thighs that twitched ever so slightly in anticipation of his touch. He'd pay for this one, that was for sure. But no power on heaven or earth could stop him from making love to her tonight.

She reached for him, and he caught her hand, staring into her eyes as he kissed each one of her fingers.

"I want you so bad," he told her truthfully. "Like I've never wanted anything in my life."

She smiled up at him, blinking a sheen of moisture from her eyes. He stripped off his shirt, tearing most of the buttons. Then he yanked off his pants, and her eyes went wide at his naked body.

"It's been…"

He waited.

"A while," she finished.

A feeling of primal possessiveness welled up inside him. He reached for the delicate wisp of her panties and discovered his hand was shaking.

She covered his blunt fingers with her small, manicured hand. "Nervous?" she asked.

Hell no. "Trying to take it slow," he managed.

She hooked her thumbs into the lace strips at her hip bones and pulled downward. "Why?"

He blinked, transfixed by the light downy curls covering her innermost secrets. The rampage of lust that slammed into him almost knocked him over. He grasped her panties and finished the job for her. "Damned if I know."

Then he eased down atop her, kissing her deeply, urging her mouth open, capturing her tongue, while his hand worked its way down her smooth skin. He thrummed one nipple, rolling it to a peak, encouraged by the groans and moans and the wriggle of her small body under his thighs. He followed her ribcage, dipping into her navel, teasing her soft curls, feeling the puffs of her gasping breath against his ear.

Then her hands went on a journey of their own, along his side, her thumbs grazing his flat nipples, her fingertips digging into his back, just hard enough to ratchet up his desire. Then they trailed over his buttocks, to the backs of his thighs, her nails grazing his skin, circling in, starting a familiar pulse at the base of his brain.

In an act of self-preservation, he grasped her hands, dragging them up, pinning them firmly to the mattress on either side of her head. She tried to protest, but he kissed it away. He used his knee to nudge her thighs apart. Then he pulled back, ever so slightly, watching her expression as he eased his way inside.

Her lips parted, rounding in an "Oh," while her hips flexed against him. He gritted his teeth, refusing to rush, letting her heat and moisture envelope him. Though his brain screamed at him to hurry, and his hormones battled his muscles for control, he forced himself to stop, to regroup, then to carry on one centimeter at a time.

Kristy thrashed her head from side to side. She drew up her knees and pushed her hips forward. But he drew back with her, controlling the pace, holding them both on the edge of exquisite torture.

His muscles turned to molten steel, and her pleas for mercy scalded what was left of his self-control. But he didn't give in…didn't give in…didn't give—

A pithy swear word leaped from his soul, and he lunged forward, burying himself to the hilt.

She freed her hands, and her arms wrapped tight around his neck. Her lips and tongue planted hot, wet kisses along his shoulder.

His mouth was jealous, so he cupped her chin, lining her up for a carnal kiss as his body found its rhythm. He teased her tongue, sucked on her lips, tasted the sweet nectar of her mouth.

Her hands squeezed tight on his biceps, her fingernails denting his skin. Sweat formed between them, slicking their skin, adding to the eroticism of their joining. He cupped her buttocks, drawing her tight against him, tighter, tighter, as he pumped harder and faster. He could feel her muscles tense. Her mewls of desire grew higher pitched, louder against his ear.

This was it. He was losing it.

He held on, held on, held on.

Then her keening cry and the convulsions of her body sent him crashing over the edge. Waves of release washed over him as he held her, reveling in the warm buzzing glow of satiation.

Reality was going to hit them like a freight train, he knew. But, for now, nothing mattered except the small sporadic twitches that told him Kristy was resting on the same plane of satisfaction as him. He inhaled the scent of her hair, stroked his hand over her full breast, tasted the salt of her skin.

Her breathing gradually relaxed, and he eased her sleeping body into a spoon against his own. Then he reached for his cell, and sent a quick text message to Simon.

No need to head for L.A. now. Jack had accomplished his mission.

He swallowed a sudden lump in his throat, his usual self-righteousness was battling an unfamiliar and unsettling slither of guilt. He told himself it had to be done. The family was his responsibility. And, anyway, Kristy had brought it on herself.

She had.

He hadn't been given a choice.

Then she wriggled her bare bottom against him, and his arm spontaneously tightened around her. She turned her head to look up at him and smiled like an angel, even as the unmistakable glow of desire rose in her blue eyes.

He chuckled softly, brushing a lock of hair from her flushed cheek. "Again?"

She nodded, and he immediately kissed her swollen mouth.

His body sprang to attention. He flipped her onto her back, pressing her warmth and softness into the big, wide mattress. Just a little longer, he promised himself as desire and passion licked at the corners of his soul. Just a few more hours in paradise.

He'd be burning in hell soon enough.

Six

Jack was awakened by Kristy's cry of shock. She scooted out of his arms, flipping back the covers and letting in a blast of cold air.

He blinked his blurry eyes to see her leap from the bed and rush naked into the en suite.

"What?" he called out, sitting up and ruffling his hands through his messy hair. He could see her naked profile at the sink as she scrambled for the toothpaste. They'd made love into the early-morning hours, then slept soundly in each other's arms. She couldn't be shocked to find herself naked in his bed this morning.

She marched from the bathroom, a white robe draped around her shoulders, open in front, a toothbrush protruding from her mouth. She unceremoniously uncovered him. "We're late!"

Jack rolled out of bed, slipping his arms into the other robe as a concrete block settled firmly in his stomach. They weren't late, because they weren't going to her meeting in California, and it was time for him to 'fess up. He couldn't postpone it any longer.

She trotted back to the sink, spitting out the toothpaste and rinsing her mouth. "Call Simon," she commanded, above the sound of the running water. "Tell him to warm up the engines or something."

Jack tried to frame up his confession, but he couldn't find the correct words. Hell, he could barely command his vocal chords to work.

"Kristy," he finally rasped.

She turned. "Why are you still standing there?"

His hands involuntarily closed into fists. "Because there's no point in going to L.A."

Her glance shot to the clock on the bedside table. It showed eight-fifteen, and her voice went hollow. "We could call Cleveland and explain."

Jack jerked backward, his guilt turning to shock. "*Explain* that we got married?"

She nodded.

"And you think he'll still want to see you?"

Her eyes went wide, giving her face a sweet, vulnerable look that almost got to him. But he ruthlessly reminded himself who she was and what she'd planned, and that she'd married him under as many false pretenses as he'd married her.

"He values punctuality that much?"

Jack shook his head, giving a dry chuckle. "I think he values fidelity that much."

"Huh?"

"Kristy, you married me." Jack jammed his thumb against the center of his chest. "*Me,* not him."

She blinked, and her voice dropped to a confused whisper. "What are you talking about?"

Man, she was good. Sometimes he couldn't believe just how good she was. He also couldn't believe she'd keep the dumb act up for this long. What was the point?

He grabbed his slacks from the chair where he'd tossed

them last night. He stuffed in one leg and then the other, watching her with a fatalistic curiosity.

"The jig is up, babe. You can't get your hands on Cleveland's money if you're already married to me. And you can't get your hands on mine because, one of those papers you signed last night was a pre-nup. And it'll hold up in court."

Kristy staggered back. For a second there, he thought her knees might give out beneath her. *"What?"*

"What?" he mimicked, sarcastically even as he fought the urge to pull her into his arms and offer comfort.

He hated himself for that weakness. And because of his inner battle, the response came out harsher than he intended. "You're caught. You're not going to be Mrs. Trophy-Wife-Cleveland-Osland-Number-Three. You'll have to find another scheme to hawk those rags you call a spring collection."

Her face turned pure white, and she groped to steady herself on the back of a chair.

Then his cell phone jangled on the table. He snagged it, hoping it was an emergency that would get him out of here and away from his unreasonable guilt.

"Yeah?" he barked.

"Where the hell are you?" his grandfather's voice boomed.

Perfect. Could the moment get any worse?

"Vegas," Jack answered, while Kristy blinked at him with big, round, accusatory, blue eyes. He was tempted to turn away from her censure. But he was in the right. She was the one who'd hatched the plan to get his family's money.

He held his ground.

"Hunter tells me you've got Kristy."

"Yeah," said Jack, holding her gaze. "The two of us got married last night."

"Well, get your asses to California. I've got seven people sitting around the boardroom table waiting for her."

Gramps reaction threw Jack. "Didn't you hear me? We *got married* last night."

"Bully for you. Nanette and I bought a Ferrari last night."

"Who's Nanette."

"My fiancée."

The sensation of being sucker-punched was so strong that Jack actually flinched.

He stared at Kristy in horror as she held the oversized robe around her for protection—her confused eyes, her sleep-mussed hair, her over-kissed lips.

What had he done?

What *had* he done?

Stupid question.

He'd married the wrong woman.

Hearing Jack's explanation, and listening to his side of the telephone conversation with Cleveland, it took Kristy about thirty seconds to put the pieces together. The whole thing was a fraud. Jack hadn't been falling in love with her this weekend. He'd been making a preemptive strike against her.

Her feelings of hurt, confusion and embarrassment were quickly replaced by anger. What kind of a cold, calculating snake did it take to fake a romance, marry a woman and then make love to her, not once, not twice, but *three times?*

Jack snapped his phone shut, and they stared at each other in silence for a long second.

"We'll get a divorce," he pronounced.

"You bet your life we'll get a divorce." She yanked the belt tight on the robe. "Although keeping your hands to yourself last night and leaving open the option for an annulment would have been a nice touch."

"I couldn't take that chance."

Her bark of laughter came out a little high-pitched. "Of course you couldn't take that chance, what with me being a sleazy gold digger and all. *Any* reasonable man would have had sex with me so I couldn't get an annulment."

"Kristy—"

"Don't you *dare* try to defend yourself."

"It's happened before."

She looked him up and down. "What? You've married other women who were engaged to your grandfather?"

"No! I mean he—"

"I don't want to hear about it."

"He's married bimbos—"

"Stop."

"—before!" Jack shouted over her protest.

A *bimbo?* That's what he thought of her?

She coughed out a harsh laugh. It was either that or cry.

"Well, in that case, Jack. You came up with a great plan. I mean, if you take away morals and ethics and, well, every scrap of reasonable humanity. It was a great plan."

"I thought you were—"

"A bimbo. Uh-huh. You've made that clear. So, is my meeting in L.A. still on or what?"

"This afternoon."

"Good." She stomped back to her own room, intending to call an airline and book a commercial flight. If she never saw Jack Osland again, it would be far too soon.

"You take the jet." His voice was directly behind her.

"Get out of my bedroom."

"You take the jet," he repeated. "Simon is ready. I'll make other arrangements."

"Don't do me any favors."

"It's the least I can do."

"Under the circumstances, there is no least you can do."

"It's the only way for you to get there on time."

She sucked in a breath between her clenched teeth. He was probably right, and maybe she was a fool to strive for any scrap of dignity at this point anyway. The man had kissed every inch of her body last night. And she'd told him she loved him.

A sharp pain pierced her chest.

She truly thought she had.

"Fine," she bit out. "I'll take the damn jet. But only as long as you're not on it." Then she turned away from him to jerk open a dresser drawer and plucked out the skirt and sweater she'd arrived in.

"Don't take this the wrong way, Jack" she said. "No. Actually. Go ahead and take it the wrong way if you like. But I never want to see you again."

"Understandable," he muttered.

She twisted around to look at him. "Gee, thanks."

"I had my reasons," he said.

"It was a great plan," she mocked. "You must be really disappointed that it failed."

One look at the expressions on the Sierra Sanchez buying team told Kristy she was going to fail.

Her sketches littered the top of the polished mahogany boardroom table, with swatches and samples draped on racks around them.

"The lines are technically strong," said one of the men. She thought his name was Bernard.

"The fabric works, but it'll be a challenge for the skirt to stand out in a crowd." Irene Compton was the lead buyer for the chain.

"Overall," said the one named James, sifting through her sketches like greeting cards. "The collection is… competent."

Kristy felt herself shrinking in the luxurious armchair. Competent. Thousands and thousands of budding designers were competent. She didn't have a hope unless she was outstanding.

"Hmm," Irene nodded. "Maybe we could think about testing it in Value-Shoppe?" She named a European discount chain.

Value-Shoppe? Kristy had to bite down on her tongue to keep from protesting out loud.

The room went silent, while each of the team members contemplated the drawings. Bright yellow sunshine streamed through the window. Car horns honked a dozen stories below, and a mist of clouds gathered in the distance over the bay. The world outside was still spinning, even while her dreams were being dashed.

"Well, *I* think she shows promise," said Cleveland.

Six jaws snapped shut, and everyone's attention flew to the older man sitting at the head of the table.

Seconds of silence ticked by before Cleveland spoke again. "I was thinking about the Breakout Designer category at the Matte Fashion Event."

Adrenaline hit Kristy's system in a rush at the mere mention of the prestigious London fashion show. A designer couldn't even enter the Breakout Designer Contest without a powerhouse retailer behind her. Even in her wildest dreams…

"Perhaps if we mix and match some of the ideas," Irene offered slowly, glancing at a patterned skirt and a white lace blouse.

Cleveland nodded his approval. "Now you're getting creative."

Kristy didn't want Cleveland's charity. But the *Breakout Designer category?* She swallowed her common sense, and let the conversation carry on around her.

Bernard jumped in. "This neckline is unique. And we can certainly scallop the hem and slim down the line."

"We'd need at least a half-dozen new or revamped pieces for the contest," James warned.

Cleveland brought the flat of his palms down on the tabletop. "That's fine. Since we're all on board, you can talk through the details later." His attention turned to Kristy. "Right now, Kristy is joining me for a drink."

She glanced at the buying team, bracing herself for narrow-eyed glares and sidelong expressions of condemnation. They might all think the way Jack did—that Kristy was Cleveland's floozy. Why else would he overrule their judgment on her behalf?

But, to her surprise, everyone was smiling.

Irene rose from her chair and offered her hand. "We're looking forward to working with you, Kristy."

The other team members nodded and murmured agreement.

Kristy stood up to shake hands with Irene. "Uh. Thank you."

Cleveland opened the boardroom door. "This way, young lady."

She nodded her thanks to the rest of the team, then preceded Cleveland into the wide, bright, plant-adorned hallway.

"You didn't have to do that," she said as they made their way to the bank of elevators.

"Do what?"

She motioned behind them, torn between being polite and shutting the heck up. "Back there. Give me special—"

"You think I pulled rank because I like you?"

"Well…"

He pressed the elevator button with a wrinkled finger. "Kristy, I've made a whole lot of money in my life by seeing things that other people miss. You have something. It's raw, but I think it's there.

"I'll work with you," he continued. "And I'll buy your collection when and if it's good enough. But that back there wasn't altruism and it wasn't nepotism."

A flutter of excitement rolled through Kristy's stomach. Cleveland actually thought her fashions had a chance?

"It's going to take a lot of work and dedication."

She eagerly nodded. She'd work as hard as it took for a chance to fly to London and compete in the Breakout Designer Contest.

"Are you prepared for that?"

"Of course."

"We have until December thirtieth."

Kristy quickly did the math in her head. That was less than three days per outfit. Impossible. But she'd have to do it anyway. "Right."

"Your staff is available over the holidays?" he asked.

Kristy hesitated. Not because her staff might not be available, but because she didn't actually have any staff.

"Kristy?"

The elevator pinged, and the doors slid open.

She took a step forward. "Don't worry. I'll manage."

"Kristy."

She didn't look up at him. "Yes?"

"How many people work for you?"

She swallowed as the doors glided shut.

Cleveland waited.

"Just me," she finally squeaked.

There was a long silence as the car glided downward and floor numbers flashed red.

"You've got guts," said Cleveland. "I'll give you that. But if this is going to work, you must be completely honest with me."

"Sorry."

"How big is your workshop?"

"It takes up most of my loft."

He raised a gray, bushy eyebrow. "Don't be evasive."

"It's six hundred square feet."

The elevator eased to a stop.

"Well that's definitely not going to do it," said Cleveland, gesturing for her to move ahead of him into the lobby.

As they walked across the polished marble floor, past statues and paintings, skirting a central waterfall encircled by bench seats, Kristy could feel the deal of a lifetime slipping from her grasp. She couldn't really blame Cleveland. Six outfits in three weeks was nearly impossible under the best of conditions. But it seemed downright cruel of fate to bring her this close, to tantalize her with the brass ring, only to unceremoniously yank it away from her.

"You'll come work at the mansion," said Cleveland decisively.

Kristy stopped in her tracks. What mansion? *His* mansion? The Osland family mansion?

He halted and turned back, a sly smile coming over his wrinkled face. "Really. You're married to Jack now. You have every right to spend the holidays with his family. We have a lovely estate in Vermont, near Manchester."

Kristy didn't even know where to start. She wasn't married to Jack. Well, she was. But she wasn't. At least not in any real sense. And she never wanted to see him again. She sure wasn't about to arrive on his doorstep for the holidays.

"That's insane," she finally managed.

"Excuse me?" said Cleveland, his bushy eyebrows slanting in an expression of surprise.

Whoops. For a minute she'd forgotten who she was speaking to.

"Sorry," she offered.

He gave her a sharp nod. "There's a workshop. Plenty of room for you to spread out. And we can bring in machines, materials and staff."

Kristy hesitated, worried about making him angry. But they had to get the matter at hand out in the open.

"You *do* know why Jack married me, right?" She might be embarrassed about being duped, but she had promised Cleveland she'd be completely honest with him. And, on this, she definitely needed to be honest.

"Certainly I know why he married you. They think because I'm eighty, I'm losing my marbles."

His bluntness surprised her.

"Are you?" she dared to ask.

He sobered, and the sound of the indoor waterfall filled the silence around them.

"No," he said. "I'm running out of time. I like beautiful young women. And I'm running out of time."

Her stomach clenched with worry. "Are you…ill?"

He shook his head and smiled. "Just old." Then he straightened, taking command once again. "But I'm still the major shareholder. This is your choice, young lady. You can work through the holidays in Vermont, or I can find someone else to sponsor for the Breakout Designer Contest."

"And Jack?"

A twinkle came into Cleveland's eyes. "You're worried Jack won't want to see you?"

She was more worried that she didn't want to see him. But the other had certainly crossed her mind. She and Jack had parted with some pretty harsh words. Still, it didn't mean she'd let him ruin her career.

Watching the play of emotions across her face, Cleveland patted her shoulder reassuringly. "I think my grandson deserves to reap the consequences of his actions, don't you?"

And then she got it, she understood Cleveland's motivation for inviting her to the family mansion. "I'm your revenge on Jack."

"Nice little twist, isn't it?"

"He was trying to protect you, you know." Even as the words popped out, Kristy couldn't believe she was defending the man. He'd manipulated, hurt and humiliated her for his own ends. He was a cold-hearted snake, nothing more.

"And what makes you think I'm not trying to help him?" asked Cleveland.

"Because there's nothing about me being in Vermont that will help Jack."

"Well then, what about becoming a successful fashion designer and winning this year at the Matte Fashion Show?"

Kristy paused. "And I should do everything in my power to make sure that happens, shouldn't I?"

"If you have a single brain cell in your pretty head, then yes."

"I do," she said.

"Then we understand each other."

She couldn't help but smile in admiration. "Your marbles are fully intact, aren't they?"

"That they are. But it suits me sometimes to let people think otherwise." He gestured towards the glass doors leading to the street. "Shall we get that drink now?"

Kristy started walking. "You know what I think?"

"What do you think?"

"That Jack learned everything he knows from you."

"Let's hope you're wrong about that."

* * *

"So I guess we got it wrong," said Hunter, looking more amused than worried as he teed off on the first hole at Lost Links. He watched as the ball arced down the fairway, bouncing to rest just shy of the horseshoe-shaped sand trap and a small grove of oaks.

"We damn sure got it wrong," said Jack, accepting the one wood from his caddy. His mood had been foul for two days now. "And I blame *you* for the screw-up."

"Me?"

"It was your brilliant idea to date her."

"I wanted to date her because she was hot, not in some Machiavellian attempt to thwart Gramps's wedding."

"Don't knock Machiavelli." Planning and strategy were the watchwords of every executive.

"I noticed you didn't deny she was hot."

"All right, she's hot. But she was dating our grandfather."

"No, she wasn't."

"Well, she could have been." Jack pushed his tee into the turf then straightened. He'd gone over and over his weekend in Vegas, wondering why he'd never once questioned Kristy's identity. Even with all the little inconsistencies in her behavior, he'd never once asked himself that pivotal question. He hated making mistakes.

"If she had been dating him," he felt compelled to point out to Hunter. "It would have been a good plan."

Hunter peered down the sunny fairway. "With a solid plan like that, it's almost hard to believe anything went wrong."

"Yeah," Jack agreed as he lined up to tee off.

He thwacked the ball dead on, and it sailed over the treetops, bouncing into the center on the fairway only a few feet short of the green.

Hunter waited for Jack to hand over the club to his caddy. "So, explain to me why we'll lose less money with you married to her instead of Gramps."

"Because I had her sign a prenup. You think I'm stupid?"

"You really want me to answer that today?"

"Get stuffed." Jack pulled off his white leather glove and turned to head down the fairway. He'd spend years living this one down.

Hunter fell into step beside him, the two caddies staying several paces behind. "Let me make sure I'm understanding this. In a haze of passion, on a lark, at the hotel chapel, she agrees to marry you, and you pull out a prenup. She didn't find that odd?"

Jack was trying hard not to think about the hotel chapel, nor the lies he'd told her to get her there. "There were other things to sign. And she wasn't paying all that much attention to the details."

"Because you're irresistible to women?"

Yeah, right. "It's a curse."

Hunter's laughter rumbled across the quiet golf course. "My sympathies. So, what now?"

Jack shrugged. "Now we get divorced."

"Just like that?"

"I suspect she's called her lawyer already."

"You don't think she's going to sue your ass?"

"Based on what? Showing poor judgment in Vegas? If that was grounds for action, our legal system would be gridlocked into the next century." No, Jack was pretty sure he was safe on the financial front.

Hunter stopped next to his ball, sizing up the lay of the course and checking the direction of the wind rustling through the palm fronds. "So, that's that?" he asked Jack, then glanced at his caddy with his brow raised.

"Six iron," the young man suggested.

"Not exactly," said Jack. "Gramps is still engaged to Nanette."

"Well, you can't marry them all," said Hunter.

Jack's marrying days were definitely over. "I wasn't thinking about me."

Hunter lined up his shot. "Look into my eyes," he said

matter of factly, with a swing and follow through. He went to stand directly in front of Jack. "Not with a gun to my head."

"I'm sure she's a knockout."

"And I'm sure you've lost your mind." Hunter handed the club back to his caddy, and they all started for the spot where Jack's ball lay.

"You got a better plan?" asked Jack.

"I've got a thousand of them. And none of them involve me marrying anybody."

"He marries Nanette, it'll cost us."

"There are more important things in life than money."

As they made their way over the fine-trimmed grass, Jack pondered the relative value of money and emotional health. He'd never really thought about it before because money had always been paramount. But if his wakefulness the last two nights was anything to go by, money had some serious competition. He wished he'd put Kristy on a commercial plane the minute they hit Vegas.

He didn't need the stress of worrying about how she was feeling, nor of his conflicted memories, nor of dwelling on the prediction of a long-ago gypsy. Which, by the way, was beginning to feel like a curse.

The curse of the midnight gypsy. It would make a good movie title. Hunter could be the hero. Jack the villain. Kristy would get rich, and the redheaded girl would be adored by fans around the world.

He lined up on the ball, chipping it up onto the green, less than ten feet from the hole.

"So, whatever happened to Vivian?"

Hunter glanced up sharply. "Huh?"

"She was the redhead, right?"

Hunter stared at Jack as if he'd lost his mind.

"A couple of years ago. You dated that redhead who beat the crap out of you at golf."

"Only because she used the ladies' tee."

"So, you do remember."

Hunter shrugged, snagging his putter and walking onto the green. "Sure."

"Where is she now?"

Hunter crouched down on one knee, eyeing the slope of the terrain. "Why do you care?"

"You remember when you burned down the gypsy's tent?"

Hunter stood up. "You mind if I play golf now?"

"Seriously," said Jack.

"No. I've forgotten the rampaging elephants, the fire department and the lawsuit that grounded me for a month."

Jack grinned, his mood lightening for the first time in forty-eight hours.

"You remember what she said?"

"How did this get to be about me?"

"She said a redheaded girl would give you twins."

Hunter shook his head in disgust and turned to address the ball.

Jack held his tongue while Hunter swung the putter.

The caddy lifted the flag, and the ball plunked into the hole.

"She also said I would marry a woman I didn't trust," said Jack. "Think about it, Hunter. What were the odds?"

Hunter slid the putter through his grip, handing it upside down to his caddy. "Please don't let the shareholders hear you talking like this. They'll have you impeached."

Jack stared hard at his cousin. "You remember what else she said."

"That you'd buy a golf course." Hunter glanced around. "You bring your checkbook?"

"Don't play dumb."

Hunter snorted. "I don't need to. You're doing a fine job of that all by yourself. You're a logical man, Jack. I didn't marry Vivian. There are no twins. And gypsies can't predict the future."

Maybe not consistently, but the two Jack had talked to were sporting pretty good averages. And the first one had also predicted Jack and Hunter would blow the family fortune. "Are we over-leveraged on anything?"

"No. Now hit the ball."

"Nothing out there that can bite us in the ass?"

"Not unless Kristy signed the lamest prenup ever."

Jack took a deep breath, running the cool shaft of his putter across his palm and settling his grip on the black, perforated rubber. Hunter was right. The prenup was fine. Kristy took away what she brought to the marriage, and Jack took away what he brought. Which was exactly the way he wanted it.

He took a few swings, testing the weight of the putter. Then he tapped the ball.

It followed the contour of the green, arcing up the high side then veering at the last second to hit the hole. *Exactly* the way he wanted it.

Seven

As she marched up the impossibly imposing brick steps at the Osland mansion outside Manchester, Dee Dee trotting along on her leash, Kristy reminded herself that nothing had changed. Recognition and success in the fashion world were still her dream.

She'd already had plenty of other setbacks over the years. And every time, she'd picked herself up, dusted herself off and redoubled her effort to bring her fashions to the attention of the industry.

Now, gazing up at the sprawling, three-story, snow-covered Colonial, she assured herself this was no different. She'd pick herself up one more time. Marrying Jack was merely a blip on her road to success, and a year from now she'd be laughing at the absurdity of thinking she was in love after only two days. Nobody fell in love that fast. She'd been swept off her feet by a man who'd set out to trap her. That was all.

Of *course* he'd seemed like the perfect man. Anybody could pretend to be perfect for two days. He'd laughed at her jokes, pretended to admire her intelligence, professed to like the same wines and catered to her every whim.

But it had all been a lie, a sham. And as soon as he'd shifted to the real Jack, she hadn't liked him at all. In fact, she'd hated him then. She still did. And that was why showing up on his doorstep and cornering him with his fake marriage was going to be so easy.

In the back of the limo, halfway between the airport and the Osland estate, she'd realized she wasn't simply getting revenge for Cleveland. She was also doing it for herself. Jack was in line for a comeuppance, and her success would show him a thing or two about judging people.

"And it will be his own darn fault," she pointed out to Dee Dee as she reached to ring the bell.

It chimed a musical tune, echoing inside the huge house.

A dark-haired, middle-aged woman opened the door. She wore a blue-and-white tunic with slim gray slacks. Her glance flicked to Dee Dee then returned to Kristy.

"Can I help you, ma'am?" she asked pleasantly.

"I'm here to see Jack Osland."

The woman stepped back, opening the door wide. "Mr. Osland is expecting you?"

Kristy shook her head.

The woman's smile faltered for a scant second. "Who shall I tell him is calling?"

Kristy stepped over the threshold. Dee Dee followed, her trimmed nails making muted clicks on the black-and-white tile.

"His wife," said Kristy.

The woman's brown eyes went round for a moment. "I'm sorry?"

Kristy nodded in confirmation of what the woman had just heard. "You can tell him his wife is…home."

"Fine." With admirable aplomb, the woman gestured to a gilt settee along one oak wall of the bright, octagonal room. "Please, do have a seat."

"Thank you," said Kristy, as the woman exited down a long hallway. She walked over to the settee with Dee Dee trotting along beside her. Instead of sitting down, she scooped the dog into her arms, straightening Dee Dee's blue, satin-lined coat. It was made of fleece, with a discreet appliqué sewn at the collar. She gave the dog a reassuring pat, snuggling it close to her chest.

It took about thirty seconds for swift, masculine footsteps to sound on the hardwood floor of the hallway.

Kristy took a deep breath, squaring her shoulders as Jack rounded the corner.

When he saw her, he came to an abrupt halt. Sunbeams from the beveled windows shone in his dark eyes, highlighted the uncompromising planes and angles of his clean-shaven face.

"Is this a joke?" he demanded.

She kept her voice light and airy by sheer force of will. "Hello, honey."

His square jaw clenched in the booming silence that followed her words.

"I'm home," she finished.

He advanced warily, as if Dee Dee might bite. Which was ridiculous.

"This isn't your home," he stated.

"I'm your wife."

"In name only."

"Actually, if you'll recall, your name was pretty much the only thing I didn't take."

"What do you want?"

"Domestic bliss."

"I'm serious."

"So am I."

"If this is about money—"

"This is about fashion."

He rolled his eyes and made a sound of disbelief deep in his chest.

Another figure emerged from the hallway. "*There* you are." Cleveland strode across the foyer, his hands outstretched.

Jack jerked back in reaction.

"We were getting worried," said Cleveland, scooping Dee Dee out of Kristy's arms and planting a dry kiss on Kristy's cheek.

"Gramps," Jack interrupted.

"Did I forget to mention Kristy was coming?" the old man asked Jack, his face a picture of innocence. Kristy didn't buy it for a second.

Then all of Cleveland's attention turned to Dee Dee. "There's my sweet Pookie," he cooed, holding the dog aloft and letting her lick his nose. To Jack he said, "Don't just stand there, my boy. Get the suitcases."

"She's not staying," Jack quickly put in.

"She is. She's your wife."

"This isn't a joking matter. If she moves in—"

"I've offered Kristy the use of the workshop above the garage."

Kristy watched Jack's eyes narrow, small creases appearing in the corners. "Why?"

"To prepare for the Breakout Designer Contest at the Matte Fashion Event in London. Sierra Sanchez is sponsoring her."

Jack shot Kristy an accusatory glare.

The man could certainly be intimidating, but she refused to back down. She wouldn't, not after coming this far. Still, she didn't want to fight in front of Cleveland. So she arranged her features in a picture of naïveté. "Would you mind showing me to my room?" she asked Jack.

"Great idea," said Cleveland, tucking Dee Dee into his arm like a football. "By the way, Nanette and I have called it quits. She's keeping the ring. And the Ferrari as a matter of fact."

With that, the older man strode from the foyer.

Jack's dark gaze bore into Kristy. "How did you do it?"

She couldn't resist. "The same way Nanette did it?"

"Kristy," he growled.

"I showed him my clothes, Jack. Not that it's any of your business."

· "This family is my business."

Okay. She wasn't going to do this. He was one powerful and sexy man, and he clearly wasn't used to being crossed.

Not that she was crossing him. Quite the contrary. He was the one who'd crossed her. But she suspected it would be a cold day in hell before he'd admit it.

She tipped up her chin. "I think I'll check out the workshop. I've got a lot to do."

"This is about revenge, isn't it?"

She barked out a cold laugh. "Don't flatter yourself. If not for the career opportunity, I wouldn't have given you another thought for the rest of my life."

She was lying. She'd lain awake four nights running remembering him.

The workshop was a dream come true. Kristy had been expecting something dark and dusty, since it was above the garage, which was separate from the house. Instead, the room was bright and sparkling, with high ceilings and freshly painted white walls. A bank of windows lined one wall of the huge, rectangular room, while fluorescent lights gleamed off the hardwood floor. It had five oversized, white-topped tables, at least a dozen utility chairs, several padded stools and a long bank of closets stretching from one end to the other.

While she struggled to keep her jaw from dropping open, Jack crossed his arms over his chest. "Tell me again how this isn't about revenge."

She snapped herself back to reality. "I don't have to explain myself to you."

"I'm the one footing your bill."

"Your grandfather's footing my bill. He's also the one getting revenge."

Jack drew back in surprise. "You're Gramps's revenge on me?"

"Either that or I'm a brilliant fashion designer. Take your pick."

Jack gave a snort of disbelief.

"Thanks so much for the vote of confidence."

"I'm going with the mathematical odds."

"Well, I'd give it a thousand to one that I'm staying."

"You can't stay."

"Oh, yes I can." She was planting her butt in this dream of a workshop and getting ready for the most prestigious fashion contest in the world.

"My mother will be here tomorrow."

"So?"

"So, I am *not* about to explain a wife over the garage."

"I take it she doesn't know about your preemptive marriage?"

"Of course she doesn't know."

"Then you might want to come up with a cover story." Kristy turned away, running her fingers over the smooth tabletop, meandering her way through the room.

"I get it," said Jack with a frustrated sigh. "Go ahead. Tell me what it'll take?"

"For me to disappear?"

"Of course."

"Nothing."

"Really?"

"I mean there's nothing you can offer. Nothing I want." Other than what she had here. She had exactly what she wanted right here. Except for Jack's oppressive presence, obviously.

"Everybody wants something," he said.

"Maybe. But I've already got it."

"Do you want an apology? Is that it?"

She turned back. "An apology would have been nice four days ago."

"Okay, I'm sorry. I'm sorry I misjudged you. I'm sorry I married you."

"What you mean is that you're sorry you're stuck with me."

"Can you be reasonable for a minute?"

"I don't think so."

Jack gave a hard sigh.

"You made your bed," she pointed out.

"And I made a pretty damn fine bed for you while I was at it."

"And I'm lying in it."

His jaw tightened, and they stared at each other in crackling silence.

But, despite her best efforts, her sympathies were engaged. She had a mother, too.

"You don't have to tell her we're married," she finally suggested.

"You announced it to the staff," he reminded her.

"Oh, yeah." She paused. "Bad luck."

"That makes this partly your fault."

"*That's* the tack you want to take?"

He'd had her there for a second, but he was quickly losing the advantage. This wasn't her problem. It was his. And she didn't need to feel any obligation to solve it for him.

But then he had the grace to look sheepish, and she felt bad again. And his motives, after all, were honorable. He was trying to help his grandfather. Kristy had merely been collateral damage.

"We could tell her the truth," she offered. "We had a whirlwind relationship in Vegas."

"And how do I explain that you're in the guest room?"

"I didn't work out? We had a fight?"

He advanced on her. "That'll just raise more questions."

"Well, we're running out of options here." She was trying to be helpful, but he wasn't making it easy.

"Not quite."

"What do you mean?"

"We pretend we're happily married. Then we pretend we divorce in a month or so."

Kristy shook her head. That sounded like way too much Jack, and way too often. "I don't think so."

He glanced around the big room. "Name your price."

"I already told you, I don't have a price."

"Fabric? Notions? Sewing machines?"

"Cleveland beat you to it."

"A staff?" Jack continued. "An unlimited budget."

"No."

"Do you have any idea what an unlimited budget means in my world?"

"You mean the world where you own private jets and rent helicopters?"

He nodded. "That world."

She wasn't sure if it was his apology, the expression in his eyes or the thought of an unlimited budget. But, she hesitated.

"Do you want to win the contest?" asked Jack.

Sure, she wanted to win. Her life would change overnight if she won.

His voice dropped to a conspiratorial level. "I can make that happen."

"You can't bribe the judges." What kind of a victory would that be?

Jack rolled his eyes. "I'm not bribing anybody. I can get you silk from the Orient, wool from Kashmir, lace from France, and I can fly you to the corners of the earth to pick it all out."

Kristy was human enough to be tempted.

And Jack was smart enough to seize the moment. He held out his hand.

She narrowed her eyes, wanting to make sure their cards were on the table. "And I'd have to…?"

"Smile at parties, sip champagne, wrap a few gifts and skate on the pond." Then his gaze went dark and his voice turned husky. "And sleep in my bed, of course."

A rush of heat burst in her chest.

"Purely platonic, I promise," he quickly added.

"You've lied to me before," she pointed out.

"True enough." He inched closer. "But I'm not lying this

time. I'll keep my hands off, and the world is yours for the taking."

Kristy's instincts screamed at her to say yes. She was probably crazy. In fact, she was sure she was crazy. But he'd apologized, and he didn't really seem like a bad guy. And the things she could do with an unlimited budget....

Fate was smiling on her.

In fact, fate was flat-out grinning at her.

"Deal," she said, before she could change her mind. Then she reached out to shake his hand.

Later that evening, Jack stopped in the open door of Cleveland's study. "You," he said to his grandfather, "are a scheming and manipulative old man."

Cleveland glanced up from where he was cooing at the goofy little dog. "Unlike you?"

"You brought her here on purpose."

"I brought her here to design clothing."

Jack shook his head, advancing into the room, past the leather sofa, the grandfather clock and the stone fireplace, to get to the mahogany bar, which jutted out from an oak-paneled wall. "You did not. And this fashion contest is going to be a total embarrassment for Sierra Sanchez."

"Not necessarily," said Cleveland.

"Yes, necessarily," Jack countered. Plucking a gorgeous woman out of obscurity and throwing her onto the world fashion stage had about a million-to-one chance of being successful.

"Well, *I* really like her," said Cleveland.

"You really like all hot women under the age of thirty-five."

Cleveland smiled. "At least I don't marry them."

Jack poured himself a snifter of brandy. "Actually, Gramps, you do."

"As usual, you're exaggerating. All Nanette got was a sports car, a mink coat and a diamond ring." Cleveland ruffled the fur between the dog's ears. "Wasn't that all she got, Pookie?"

Jack took a seat in a leather armchair, frowning at the dog. His grandfather had always had a soft spot for animals. Though Jack had never seen him quite this attached to one before.

"You should make a go of it with Kristy," said Cleveland. "She's a great girl."

Jack coughed out a laugh. "That's a perfect idea. Because we've obviously set such a good foundation for a long-term relationship."

A telltale twinkle came into Cleveland's eyes. "So, have you decided what you're going to tell your mother?"

Jack gave him a smug smirk in return. "That it was a whirlwind romance. Kristy's agreed to play along."

"Really." Cleveland looked surprised.

Jack nodded his answer, swirling the amber liquid against his warm palm.

"And what did that cost you?"

Jack paused. "More than Nanette's sports car. Less than the condo you bought for Opal."

"I knew I liked that girl."

"Irene Compton says she's mediocre."

Cleveland shrugged. "What does Irene know? I have a feel for these things."

"No you do not have a feel for these things." What Cleveland had a feel for was his libido. He might not have been dating Kristy, but he couldn't have missed the fact that she was a knockout. "Irene, on the other hand, has been in the fashion business for thirty years."

"Everybody's wrong sometime," said Cleveland.

While that might be true, Jack knew experts were right a whole lot more often than they were wrong. That's why he hired them, and that's why he paid them so well.

Irene was an expert. And since Kristy was, by Irene's account, a mediocre designer, there was a good chance she'd crash and burn at the Breakout Designer Contest.

Bad for Sierra Sanchez, and bad for Kristy. Jack frowned at both of those thoughts and took a swig of his brandy.

Hunter appeared in the doorway. "You two kids playing nice?"

"Jack's a bit snippy," said Cleveland.

"Gramps is busy playing God."

"Not God," said Gramps. Then he paused. "Yeah, okay. God it is."

Hunter chuckled and shook his head, sauntering over to the bar. "You know there are three huge vans out in the driveway?"

"I called earlier to express a few things over for Kristy," said Jack.

"Ahh, the blushing bride," said Hunter as he followed Jack's lead and poured himself a brandy.

Jack gestured to the two men with his glass. "You two remember, for the holiday season, she *is* the blushing bride."

Hunter held up his hands. "Hey, I'm not about to tell our moms what you did."

Cleveland nodded. "And I'm not about to tell them why you did it."

"Just so we're clear," said Jack. "I'll announce an amicable divorce in January."

"And Kristy's going along with this because?" asked Hunter.

"Because of the three huge vans in the driveway," replied Jack.

"See how easy it is?" asked Cleveland.

"Funny," said Hunter. "She didn't strike me as the mercenary type."

"Everybody has their price," Jack repeated.

Not that he held it against her. Kristy recognized a good thing when she saw it was all. And Jack could respect that. It wasn't as if he was buying her a sports car or a five-carat diamond she could turn around and hawk. It was in everybody's best interest for her to do well at the Breakout Designer Contest.

Cleveland rose from his chair. "So, now that the fun's over, Pookie and I are off to bed."

"You'll remember about Kristy?" asked Jack.

"Yes, I'll remember about Kristy," Cleveland harrumphed. "You think I'm going senile?"

Jack looked at Hunter, and Hunter looked at Jack.

Cleveland shook a wrinkled finger in their direction. "Don't you forget whose brain it was that built this company. An empty warehouse and a corner store. That's what I started with."

"And the family seat at the stock exchange," Hunter pointed out.

"Wasn't worth a dime in the thirties," Cleveland countered, scratching Dee Dee on the head. "Insolent young pups," he muttered. Then he left the room, his footsteps echoing down the hallway.

"He seem okay to you?" Hunter asked, folding himself into the armchair opposite Jack.

"Mostly," replied Jack. He always thought his grandfather was absentminded only when it suited him. But Jack wondered how much of it was an act, and how much of it was a sign of a failing memory.

"He broke up with Nanette," said Jack. "So, that's a plus."

"And you marrying Kristy?" Hunter asked with a self-satisfied grin. "That a plus, too?"

"That," said Jack, swirling his brandy again, "is an inconvenience."

"A gorgeous woman pretending to be your wife. Yeah, I'd call that an inconvenience, all right."

"She's not pretending," Jack corrected. For better or worse, Kristy actually was his wife.

"So, you'll be sleeping with her?" asked Hunter.

"In a manner of speaking." Jack shifted in his chair.

Hunter gave a knowing chuckle. "Now *that,* cousin, is an inconvenience."

Jack polished off his drink. "Speaking of which." He rose to his feet. "I'd better make sure she can find the towels."

"You poor, pathetic thing," laughed Hunter.

"What?"

"It's only ten-thirty."

Jack refused to react. So it was early. So he was looking forward to climbing into bed with Kristy. So sue him.

Eight

In Jack's big bedroom, Kristy gave herself a mental pep talk. Sleeping here wasn't going to be so bad. She could keep everything in perspective.

Sure, she was attracted to him. After all, he was a great-looking, sexy guy. But she was still annoyed with him for lying to her. And her annoyance would keep her from doing anything rash.

She eyed up the king-size bed. Then she checked out the love seat tucked in an alcove with a bay window that overlooked a pathway lined with winter-bare trees, each of them glowing with hundreds of white lights. In the distance, a giant evergreen rose above the garden, blinking with color, its crowning star golden against the black sky. The Oslands really went all out with Christmas decorations.

Back to the love seat. She could co-opt a pillow and blanket from Jack's bed. The love seat was on the short side, but she could make do. And it would be better than sharing the bed.

She sat on the cushions and bounced up and down. Not

bad. She leaned over to lie down, turning on her side, bending her knees in an effort to find a comfortable position.

Not perfect.

"You've got to be kidding," came Jack's voice from the doorway.

Kristy popped into a sitting position. "Just considering my options."

He clicked the door shut behind him. "You are not sleeping on the couch."

"Well, I'm not wild about sleeping in the bed."

"We're newlyweds."

She stood. "I've got news for you, Jack. The honeymoon's over."

"Not as far as my mother is concerned. And she'll be here any day."

"Your mother won't be in your bedroom."

"But the staff will be in *our* bedroom. And I have no desire to explain why my bride is sleeping on the couch."

"I'll fold up the blankets every morning."

"Not."

"Jack—"

"Me, you, bed." He punctuated his words by pointing with his index finger. "This is not optional."

"Women usually respond well to that tone, do they?"

"I don't know. I've never had to order a woman into my bed before."

Kristy moved toward him, putting some swagger into her step. "Is that what you're doing?"

"Yeah," said Jack, hot eyes following her progress. "That's what I'm doing."

She stopped in front of him. "Well, good luck with that."

"I'm not going to need luck."

"No?"

He scooped her into his arms. Before she could do anything more than gasp in surprise, he marched across the room and deposited her on top of the duvet.

"No luck required," he stated, staring down at her.

She propped herself on her elbows, trying to look affronted, even as a grin crept out. "You cheated."

He grinned in return. "Who cares? I won."

"And how much satisfaction is there in that if you cheated?"

He leaned down, bracing a hand on either side of her, bringing their faces close together. "Quite a bit, actually."

Kristy could feel an awareness humming through her body. "I will escape," she warned in a whisper.

He raised his eyebrows. "You think?"

"The minute you're asleep."

"Well, good luck with that," he parroted.

"I'm not going to need luck," she countered.

An hour later, Kristy realized that what she really needed was a crowbar.

Jack's arm was latched firmly around her waist, anchoring her, spoon-fashion, to his body. His breathing was deep and even, so she was pretty sure he'd fallen asleep. But his grip hadn't slacked off one bit.

She was well covered, having passed over the filmy ivory and peach negligee Jack had secretly bought her in Las Vegas in favor of an oversized T-shirt. The shirt fell past her knees and was thicker than flannel. Still, Jack's forearm was warm and intimate against her stomach.

She wasn't uncomfortable. In fact, she could have easily fallen asleep. But it was a matter of principle now. She couldn't let him win this particular war.

She wrapped her fingers around his thick wrist and pulled against his arm.

His response was to mutter in her ear and snuggle closer, drawing her buttocks tight against the cradle of his thighs, his hand slipping lower, cupping her hip bone.

She froze, willing her body to ignore the sexual signals he was sending out in his sleep.

But goose bumps rose on her skin, and a thick pulse started deep in her abdomen. She squirmed, trying to get away from the sensations. But that only made things worse. Her nightgown rode up to midthigh, and the friction of Jack's hand through the fabric of her gown made the goose bumps tingle with desire.

She squirmed again, scrunching her eyes shut and biting down on her bottom lip. Desire throbbed freely now. Her toes curled and her muscles began to clench. Her nipples tightened as his breath fanned against the back of her neck.

She straightened her legs, but that brought the back of her thighs against his hot body. Skin on skin, inch after glorious inch. Her hands curled into fists. Oh, this was going to kill her.

His hand moved, and her hips flexed involuntarily backward as a gasp escaped from her lips.

He sucked in a tight breath, and she realized he was awake.

She stilled, expecting him to say something. She was embarrassed, but, more than that, she was completely aroused.

His body hardened against her.

He gave her a few moments to protest, but then his thumb drew a lazy circle around her navel. His fingertips were still snug against her hip. She knew she should say something, knew she should stop him. But cocooned by his warmth, with the Christmas lights twinkling through the big windows and his strong body enveloping her, she couldn't bring herself to break the moment.

His lips touched the back of her neck. They parted, turning the brush into a kiss.

She really had to stop him.

If she didn't stop him right this second…

Her fists curled tighter, nails biting into her palms.

His fingertips fanned their way down her thighs. They encountered bare skin. She held her breath as they trailed their way back up.

His kisses worked their way around her neck. He kissed her ear, her jawbone, her cheek, while his fingertips brushed her downy curls.

Then he drew another strangled breath. "For God's sake, tell me no."

She tried, but she couldn't form the word.

He kissed the corner of her mouth.

She turned her head to meet him, angling her body, tipping her chin.

His gaze caught hers in the blinking red and green glow. He gently found her center, and her hips flexed in reaction.

Then his mouth was on hers, kissing her passionately, his tongue delving deeply into her mouth as his finger entered her body.

She moaned, and her thighs twitched apart.

He stretched his leg over hers, pressing her into the mattress. His hand set up a rhythm, and the world shifted to the apex of her thighs.

She tried to hang on, but he hit all the right spots. She dragged in a breath, inhaling his scent. She flicked out her tongue, tasting sweet brandy on his lips. She twisted the comforter convulsively between her fingers.

He had to stop.

This was crazy.

She was out of control.

She opened her mouth, but her words turned into a cry, and sensation shattered around her.

He held her tight, slowed his kisses, whispered something that she couldn't begin to hear around the roaring in her ears. But it sounded nice. It sounded soothing. It sounded like she didn't have to worry that she'd just let go under his caress.

And then the lights blurred and the soft bed turned into a cloud, as a warm peace settled into her very bones.

In the morning, Jack hauled himself out of bed at 6:00 a.m. He'd nearly given in to temptation last night, and he didn't want to think about what he'd do if Kristy woke up sleepy and pliant in his arms. It could go one of two ways, neither of them good, and he owed it to her to at least try to keep his word from now on.

He left her sleeping and showered down the hall. Then he took coffee into the study. It was too early on the west coast even for Lisa, so he logged on to the Sierra Sanchez computer server and hunted around himself. It took nearly half an hour to find a number for Zenia Topaz.

Jack wanted to make contact with the one person who might be able to help him help Kristy. Zenia Topaz was a top fashion designer, and her contract with Sierra Sanchez gave Jack a little leverage. Plus, they'd grown to be friends over the years.

He'd already ordered what he could think of for Kristy last night from the Manchester area. But he didn't know anything about international fashion design. He had no idea what was in and what was out, what kinds of things Kristy would need to have a running chance at the Breakout Designer Contest. Hopefully, Zenia could give him some advice.

And he wasn't only doing this for Kristy, he assured himself. He had the best interests of Sierra Sanchez in mind, as well.

"Topaz Fashion," came the cheerful answer.

"Zenia Topaz, please."

"She's expecting your call?"

"No. It's Jack Osland."

"One moment please, Mr. Osland. I'll see if she's available." The line clicked.

Jack listened to elevator music, tapping his fingers against the desktop as the minutes ticked by. He realized as he waited that he didn't spend very much of his life on hold. Other people must. Although he had to remember that Zenia hadn't been expecting his call.

The line clicked again. "Mr. Osland?" came the same voice, sounding a bit breathless and flustered this time.

"Yes?"

"Ms. Topaz will be right with you. I'm sorry, sir."

"No problem," said Jack.

Another click.

"Jack," Zenia's voice singsonged.

"Good morning, Zenia. How are things in New York?"

"Things are fabulous. The city's lit up. We've been out skating already. Are you in town?"

"I'm in Manchester. I was wondering if you could help me out."

"Absolutely, Jack. Whatever I can do."

"Sierra Sanchez is sponsoring a designer in the Breakout Designer Contest at Matte Fashion."

"Umm-hmm."

He swiveled his chair to face the window. "She's working here over the holidays, and I'd like to pick up a few things for her."

"What kind of things."

"That's the problem. I'm not sure."

"Okay…" Zenia's voice was searching.

"Fabric, notions, shoes, I don't know. I was hoping you'd have some ideas."

"Do you have her sketches?"

"Not really."

"Jack—"

"It was a last-minute thing. I think she might be building on something she has, or might be coming up with something brand-new. Gramps met her—"

"Ahhh."

"Oh. No." Jack automatically shook his head. "It's not like that." Well it *was* kind of like that. "Listen, my jet is at your disposal, as is my credit card. Can you make a few calls to your suppliers? Just send one of everything."

Zenia gave a husky chuckle. "Who is this woman?"

Jack paused. "My wife."

"No way."

"It was a whirlwind courtship."

Zenia clucked her tongue. "Like grandfather, like—"

"No! Like I said, it's nothing like that."

"Sorry."

"That's all right. Can you help me out? I want to surprise her."

Kristy could buy anything else she wanted later, but Jack couldn't help thinking they'd do better with an expert like Zenia making the choices.

Zenia was silent for a minute. "You know she's only got two weeks."

"The jet is warming up on the tarmac."

Zenia took a breath. "Okay. Tell the pilot to file a flight plan to Paris then Milan. I'll send one of my assistants along to purchase what she'll need."

"You're a goddess," said Jack.

"Yes, I am. And I want to meet this woman when I'm at the show in London."

"Actually, I can suggest something even better…."

Waking up alone in Jack's bedroom was a mixed blessing. It saved her the embarrassment of facing him after last night. But now she had to spend the day dreading the moment she'd have to face him.

Did he think she was selfish? A tease? Did he think it was his turn next? Did he have expectations for tonight?

She paced the length of the workshop, giving her head a quick shake, forcing Jack from her thoughts.

She stopped herself at the drafting table, plunked down on the stool, opened the sketch pad and stared down at Irene's notes. The Sierra Sanchez team had liked the necklines. They'd liked some of the fabrics, too.

The team's biggest complaint had been the lack of sparkle and imagination. Kristy thought she understood. Unfortunately, now she wasn't so sure.

She closed her eyes, trying to think about sparkle, imagination, maybe passion.

Oops. There was Jack again.

She could see him in the hot air balloon this time, skimming over the desert against the bright-blue sky. The balloon was round, billowing out with primary colors, bright yellow, red and blue. The lines were soft, sand rippling off in the distance, rocks polished by the foaming water, curves on the river sweeping through the valley.

In the distance, the cliffs were jagged, painted with muted stripes of brown and rust and gold. A waterfall crashed over them, hurling spray high into the air, white water bubbled at the bottom of the falls. She heard Jack's rumbling voice, his laughter, his teasing suggestion they skinny-dip. She was hit with a new sense of desire, even while the foaming water turned into billowing crinoline and the stripes from the surrounding cliffs took the shape of a bodice.

Her eyes flew open. "Wow."

She grabbed her sketchbook and began bold pencil strokes across a blank page.

A wild and exotic dress grew before her eyes—a tight, sleeveless bodice, with stripes arching into a reverse, rounded neckline. She'd use some kind of metallic in the fabric, jazzing up the earth tones. She nipped in the waist, then filled out the skirt, widening the stripes as the fabric fell to midthigh. Then she penciled in the billowing crinoline, at least six inches showing below the skirt.

Dark stockings and spike heels would give the sensuality she was looking for. It was sassy and sexy and completely different from anything she'd conceived before.

She had a sudden vision of herself wearing it, curled up on the blanket in front of the waterfall, Jack's hot gaze traveling the length of her body.

She drew a deep, shuddering breath.

Then she came back to earth, blinking at the surprising creation. It didn't look like the kind of thing Irene would like. The woman's tastes had tended toward sleek and sophisticated.

But this dress was definitely passionate. And, for better or worse, Kristy was feeling passionate.

Maybe it was frustration. Or maybe it was repressed desire. Or maybe it was simply the opulence and excess of the Osland mansion. But Kristy definitely wanted to let herself go, to find her sensual side and bring it out in jazzy, extravagant clothing.

Of course, she couldn't.

She had a sponsor. And she had a job to do.

Enough fooling around. She flipped to Irene's notes on her original sketches. She'd start with her classic cocktail dress and take it from there.

When Kristy entered the mansion many hours later, tired, hungry and pretty frustrated with her efforts, she heard voices coming from the great room. She realized the rest of Jack's family had arrived, and she was in no shape to meet any of them yet.

She darted up the stairs, grabbed a shower, blow-dried her hair and got herself into a simple white-and-silver tunic dress that shimmered as she moved. High heels gave her confidence, and she matched a pair of dangling black earrings to a dramatic necklace that highlighted the V neckline.

She heard the bedroom door open and turned to see Jack approach the en-suite.

"Ready?" he asked through the doorway.

The second she heard his voice, the night before came flooding back in all its reckless, sensual glory. She instantly realized she wasn't ready to face Jack or anybody else.

"Kristy?"

She swallowed. Should she acknowledge it? Pretend she'd forgotten? Hope he'd forgotten that she selfishly went to heaven and back in his arms?

"Kristy?" he repeated, taking a couple of steps into the room. Then he stopped behind her, gazing for a long second at her reflection in the vanity mirror.

"Please don't be embarrassed," he finally said.

What else could she possibly be?

"You were beautiful," he said softly, bringing his hands down to rest on her shoulders.

"I'm sorry," she muttered, covering her face with one hand.

A smile came into his voice. "Well, I'm sure not."

She dared to meet his eyes.

"Never," he assured her. "Not even for a second."

There was something comforting about his tone and his touch. She found herself relaxing.

"Besides," he said, giving her a squeeze, "I don't know if you noticed, but we've got bigger problems downstairs."

So much for relaxing. "I noticed," she said on a sigh.

"Then buck up," he advised. "Because your in-laws are waiting."

She nodded, finishing her lip gloss and chasing down a surge of butterflies that collected in her stomach. She reminded herself they weren't really her in-laws. She didn't have to win them over for life. All she had to do was smile, nod and try not to spill anything.

Jack gestured for her to go first. "My mother's name is Liza. My sister is Elaine. Then there's my aunt Gwen and my cousin Melanie, Hunter's sister."

Kristy repeated the names to herself as they made their way along the hall and down the main staircase. Garlands of fresh cedar adorned the railing and banisters. The charming scent filled the air.

A small group of people stood chatting in the great room. Hunter asked Jack a question as they walked through the door. Kristy could see Cleveland in a conversation in the middle of the room, a crystal tumbler in one hand, and Dee Dee parked by his feet. He was sporting a Santa hat, perched jauntily atop his head. Leaving Jack behind, she moved closer to Cleveland, then she crouched down slightly.

"Dee Dee," she sang softly to get her dog's attention.

Dee Dee raised her head, but didn't come to her feet.

"He's spoiled her," came a female voice next to Kristy.

Kristy straightened and smiled at the young woman. "I may have to leave her here when I go."

She was a brunette, twentysomething, and she arched a finely sculpted eyebrow. "You're going somewhere?"

"London," said Kristy easily. Then she held out her hand. "I'm Kristy Mahoney."

The woman gave a gentle handshake. "Not Osland?"

Kristy shook her head.

"Well, I'm Elaine Osland. We appear to be sisters-in-law."

"It's good to meet you."

"You, too." Elaine took a sip of her martini, watching Kristy closely. "I hear it was a small wedding?"

"About as small as you can get."

"In Vegas?"

"Uh-huh."

"Out of the blue I take it?"

"It was a whirlwind courtship."

"That's not like Jack."

"It's not like me, either."

"More like his grandfather."

Kristy laughed, but it sounded nervous even to her ears. "Really."

"I hear you're into fashion design."

"I am. And what do you do?"

Elaine waved a dismissive hand. "Let's talk about you."

Kristy paused. "I take it you're the interrogation committee?"

Elaine had the good grace to grin sheepishly. "That's because you haven't met my mother yet."

Kristy glanced around the room.

"In the green sequin jacket," said Elaine.

The woman's shrewd eyes met Kristy's gaze, and Kristy quickly looked away.

"Any tips?" she asked Elaine.

Elaine chuckled. "Stand up straight, don't let her intimidate you and always tell the truth."

"Are there any electrodes or heart-rate monitors involved?"

"Only if you make her suspicious."

"Suspicious of what?"

"Your motivations for marrying my brother, silly."

"I had no motivations."

"See, she's going to wonder."

"It was a crazy weekend romance in Vegas," Kristy told Elaine honestly. "He took me on a balloon ride, and I was a goner." She wasn't even lying about that part.

She felt a hand on the small of her back and knew immediately it was Jack.

"Everything okay here?" he asked.

"The electrodes haven't come out yet," said Kristy.

"We're just having a chat," Elaine put in, giving her brother a quick hug.

"You be nice," Jack warned his sister.

"I'm always nice. I hear you fell in love on a balloon ride." She cocked her head to watch his expression.

"You heard right," said Jack. "It was over the Grand Canyon, and I was charming as hell."

"Hmm," said Elaine.

"Don't 'hmm' me," Jack retorted.

Elaine glanced back and forth between the two. "Only two days?"

Jack sighed. "Back off. And tell Mom to back off, too."

Elaine snorted indelicately. "Yeah, right." She turned her attention to Kristy again. "So, tell me all about your design business."

"I mean it," said Jack.

"I'm simply making conversation," Elaine retorted.

Jack took Kristy's arm. "I'd like to introduce you to my mother." He guided her away.

"Will I do any better with her?" she whispered as they crossed the room, feeling as if she was being put in front of a firing squad.

"You're doing fine."

"I'm going with the truth. It was a whirlwind courtship in Vegas, and you were charming."

He nodded. "That works." Then he put a broad smile on his face as they approached the slender woman in the emerald-green jacket.

"Mom," he said. "I'd like you to meet Kristy."

The woman turned to face them. She was somewhere between fifty and sixty, and her hair, makeup and jewelry were obviously the products of considerable wealth. Kristy recognized the jacket as a Delilah Domtar, and the slacks as William Ping.

She was tall and beautiful, but the warmth in her eyes when she greeted Jack dimmed somewhat when she looked at Kristy.

"Kristy, this is my mother, Liza."

"It's a pleasure to meet you," said Kristy, bravely holding out a hand.

Liza looked her up and down. "The pleasure is mine, I'm sure."

The words were correct, but the tone left Kristy wanting to apologize for something.

"There you are, Kristy!" Cleveland's voice boomed. "Meeting my youngest daughter, I see."

Kristy smiled in relief, and she bent down to pick up Dee Dee, a welcome distraction. "Hello, Cleveland. Nice hat."

"Thanks. Kristy here is a genius," Cleveland said to Liza.

"I'm sure she's quite the little scholar," said Liza.

Hugging Dee Dee close, Kristy caught an apology in Jack's eyes.

"Don't get yourself in a snit," Cleveland admonished Liza.

Liza glanced at Kristy and then Jack. "An invitation to the wedding was too much to ask?"

"It wasn't really a wedding," Kristy blurted, experiencing a pang of sympathy for the woman. Her own mother would be—

Her mother.

Good Lord, her *mother.*

She turned to Jack, feeling the blood drain from her face. "I have to make a phone call."

He looked confused. "Now?"

"I'm sorry." She handed Dee Dee to Cleveland and started to move away.

Jack caught her arm to stop her.

She mouthed the words *my parents*.

He drew back, comprehension dawning in his eyes.

"Will you excuse us for a moment?" he asked the group of guests.

"Dinner is in fifteen minutes," warned Liza.

With Jack at her side, Kristy left the great room and paced to the rotunda foyer.

"This is a disaster," she hissed.

"Just tell them what we're telling everyone else."

She stopped and turned around in front of the settee. "They're my *parents*." Joe and Amy Mahoney were hard-working, generous and hopelessly romantic. Amy's wedding dress had been preserved in blue tissue paper for thirty years, waiting for either Kristy or Sinclair to find the right man. And when they sold their house in Brooklyn, instead of buying beachfront in Florida, they bought something modest, a block away, to make sure they could afford fashionable weddings for their two daughters.

He gestured back to the great room. "Who do you think we were just talking to?"

"That's different."

His lips compressed. But then his eyes unexpectedly softened. "You're right. It is. Tell me how I can help."

She looked at the floor. There was nothing he could do.

Her mother would be thrilled, *thrilled* to hear that Kristy had fallen in love. Her father would hold off until he met Jack—which would be as soon as humanly possible. Then there'd be talk of grandchildren. Her parents would emotionally engage in some big, complicated fantasy of the future. Then their hopes would be dashed when the divorce was announced.

Kristy groaned.

Jack slipped an arm around her. "It's going to be okay," he muttered. "We'll make it okay."

She shook her head in denial. It wasn't going to be okay.

It was going to be horrible. "They'll want to get on a plane. They'll want to meet you in person."

"I'll send the jet."

"They can't come *here.*"

Jack nodded. "Oh, right. That would be way too complicated." He gripped the back of his neck. "What about London?"

"London?"

"Ask them to meet us in London."

"You're not coming to London."

He paused. "Good point. Okay. How about this. Tell them you've *met* a nice man. And you're spending Christmas with him, and you'll keep them posted. That way, if they find out about the marriage, you can say we were planning to surprise them together in person. And if they don't find out, we divorce, life goes on and everybody's happy."

Kristy considered the idea.

It was a long shot. But it might work. At least it gave them a fighting chance.

Jack handed her his cell phone.

Nine

A week later, Kristy's double fashion collection mirrored double life.

On the one hand, she was plain old single, struggling Kristy Mahoney. On the other, she was Mrs. Jack Osland. Her husband was flying in fabrics and accessories from Paris and Milan, while wedding gifts arrived almost hourly from pricey boutiques around the globe. She was careful not to let herself get attached to any of the expensive silver and china, and she was leaving Jack to worry about returning it when all was said and done.

Out in the workshop, she was working on two sets of sketches and two clothing collections. One was the revamped collection developed with the help of Irene and the Sierra Sanchez team. The other was the wild fantasy clothing she'd created around her Vegas trip with Jack.

Two assistants had arrived the first morning after she'd shown up at the mansion. Local women, Isabella and Megan were both competent seamstresses and cheerful companions.

Kristy was making steady progress on the real collection during the day. In the evening though, she couldn't resist using the expensive laces and fabrics to mock up some of the fantasy pieces.

"More lace," Isabella called above the hum from Megan's sewing machine. She balanced a huge white box in her arms as she closed the door behind another delivery man.

"Look at that," Megan whistled as they opened the box.

Kristy crossed the room. The box held beaded, corded, Chantilly, metallic and colored laces.

Isabella tsk-tsked. "I sure wish we were making something with lace."

What Kristy wished was that they were *showing* something with lace. The Irene collection—as she'd begun calling it in her head—was sleek and sophisticated, where the fantasy collection was flirty and fun. Kristy would be able to use all kinds of different lace on the fantasy collection. It was just too bad nobody but her would ever see it.

She was halfway through sewing the sexy, short desert dress. For that one, the lace would be key. It had to be stiff to fill out the skirt, and the edging needed to be dramatic to draw the eye, but the detail had to mimic the frothing waterfall. Kristy smiled at the memory.

"What?" asked Isabella.

Kristy immediately erased the smile. "We'd better get back to work."

They closed the box, but Kristy didn't take her own advice. Instead of settling on a fabric for the Irene collection slacks, she gazed out the window at the delicate snowflakes catching the bare branches of maple trees.

She saw the hot-air balloon again. It morphed into striped pants made of thin nylon in the same primary colors. She'd pair that with a cropped top of blue or red or…the lace! That was it. Thin out the stripes, make the top out of lace—flat cotton eyelet perhaps. She could even use a color, or maybe colored buttons down the front of the top.

Kristy surreptitiously flipped to a blank page in her sketch book. Multicolored buttons would match the colors in the pants. The lace would tie in with the frothy skirt. She put a few bold strokes across the pages, and she was off and running.

"Kristy?" Megan's voice seemed a long way off, and Kristy realized a couple of hours had gone by. Her shoulders and hand were starting to cramp.

She looked up. "Yes?"

"We're heading out now."

Kristy nodded. "Of course. Thanks."

"We can probably do a first fitting on the blue dress tomorrow. The Harold Agency said they'd send a couple of models."

Kristy nodded again. "That's great. And the green one?"

"We can cut the silk tomorrow," said Isabella.

"Thanks, guys," said Kristy.

"See you in the morning." They waved and opened the door, nearly bumping into Hunter on their way out.

They greeted him, and he bade them goodbye, then closed the shop door after them.

"How are you holding up?" he asked, strolling over to Kristy.

She closed the sketch book of fantasy designer drawings like a guilty little secret and stood to stretch her shoulders. "Not bad."

He nodded, glancing around. "Looks like you're doing a lot of work."

"That's because I am." In fact, it was double the work it should have been. But that was Kristy's own fault. Her own, self-indulgent fault.

"You working late again tonight."

"For a while. Did you need something?"

"Gramps asked if you'd—"

The shop door burst open, cutting off Hunter's words.

Kristy blinked in astonishment at the image of her sister in a bright-green woolen coat with a matching beret.

She stood. "Sinclair? What on earth?"

Sinclair marched into the room, gesturing to Hunter with her thumb. "Is this the guy?"

"What are you *doing* here?"

Sinclair whipped off the beret, revealing her wild auburn hair. "Am I not your best friend? Your confidante? Your partner in crime?"

"Hold on," said Hunter, drawing Sinclair's attention, and her ire.

"And *you,*" she said to Hunter, marching forward. "You *married* my sister?"

The word *married* clanged in Kristy's ears. "Wait a minute. How did you—"

"The old man in the house." Sinclair kept her focus on Hunter. "Where did you meet her?"

"On my jet," said Hunter.

"Hunter, don't—"

"Money doesn't give you carte blanche," said Sinclair, pacing around him. "She has a family, people who love her. People who *deserved* to meet you, before—"

"Sinclair."

"Before I kidnapped her and dragged her off to my lair?" asked Hunter.

"There's no need to be sarcastic," said Sinclair.

"And there's no need to blitz in here like the Tasmanian Devil."

"I want some answers."

"Then shut up for a minute and listen."

To Kristy's surprise, Sinclair actually did.

"He's not my husband," said Kristy.

"Somebody looking for me?" drawled Jack from the doorway.

Sinclair spun to face him. She blinked from one man to the other.

"Jack, Hunter. This is my sister, Sinclair. Sinclair, this is my husband, Jack, and his cousin Hunter."

"Mom told me you'd met a man." Sinclair unbuttoned her long coat.

"I did."

Sinclair eyed Jack up and down. "She didn't tell me you'd married him." She pulled a cell phone from the pocket and hit a speed-dial button.

Kristy jerked forward, visions of her mother on the other end of the line. "Who are you calling?"

"The airline," said Sinclair. "I had a four-hour stopover. But clearly, I'll be staying the night."

"Is she always this bossy?" asked Hunter.

"Is he always this rude?" asked Sinclair.

"Pleasure to meet you," said Jack, advancing with his hand out.

Sinclair shook, cradling the phone against her neck. "I have a few questions."

"Me, too," said Jack. "You know how to skate?"

Before Sinclair could answer him, her phone call connected, distracting her. She listened for a few seconds, then pushed a button.

"We're skating on the pond tonight," Jack explained to Kristy. "It's a traditional thing. Mom would love to have you join us."

"I should talk to Sinclair first."

"She can talk to both of us," said Jack.

Sinclair covered the mouthpiece. "I don't really care who I talk to. As long as somebody starts talking."

"Jack and I met in Vegas," said Kristy. "It was a whirlwind courtship."

"You…*you* got married in Vegas?"

"I did."

"And this doesn't warrant a phone call?"

"We were waiting—"

"For what?"

"To tell Mom and Dad in person."

"I'm not Mom and Dad."

Kristy blew out a breath. "I know."

Jack put an arm around her. If he'd tried that when she'd first arrived at the mansion, she would have shrugged it off. Now, she reveled in the strength and comfort of his simple gesture. "I think Kristy was somewhat embarrassed. She's not normally impulsive."

"And you know what she's normally like, do you?"

"She's my wife."

Sinclair shook her head. "Hello?" she said into the phone, turning away. "Yes. I'd like to change my ticket."

"You okay?" Jack asked.

"Not really," replied Kristy.

Hunter moved closer. "You want me to get rid of her?"

Kristy couldn't help but smile. "You offering to harm my sister?"

"I meant get her out of the room," clarified Hunter.

"She'll calm down in a minute."

Sinclair finished her call.

"I'll skate if I have to," she informed Jack. "As long as somebody does some talking while I'm skating. And as long as there is some kind of alcoholic beverage at the end."

Then she moved forward and drew Kristy into a one-armed hug. "I wanted to be a bridesmaid," she muttered. "How could you do this to me?"

"Jack is persuasive," Kristy answered.

Sinclair drew back, smoothing the front of Kristy's hair. "Obviously. And I want to hear all about it."

The moon was full, the stars snapping bright, and strings of white Christmas bulbs illuminated the periphery of the glassy pond. Jack's gloved hand was tucked into Kristy's as they made lazy circles around the edge of the ice.

He could see Hunter in the distance, annoying Sinclair by skating around her as she struggled to stay on her feet. Further back was his family. Cleveland carried Dee Dee, while Elaine and Melanie laughed their way through fumbled spins and jumps.

Beside him, Kristy looked beautiful. Her cheeks were rosy beneath her fur-trimmed hat. Her lips were full and dark, and her eyes glowed indigo beneath her thick lashes.

"I seriously thought about telling her the truth," she admitted, referring to her private conversation with Sinclair at the beginning of the excursion.

"But you didn't?" Jack asked, enjoying the feel of her small hand in his. He turned and snagged the other, skating backward so they were facing each other.

She sighed. "I stuck with our story."

The urge to lean forward and kiss her was so strong. "Will she tell your parents?" he asked instead.

Kristy shook her head. "She promised me she'd wait and let me tell them in person."

"That's good."

"There's nothing at all good about this."

"I disagree."

"How can you disagree? The whole damn world thinks we're married."

He shrugged, not really caring what anybody in the world thought. It was getting harder and harder to regret spending time with Kristy. In fact, he was getting greedy for more of it. She was working such long hours on the collection. He was proud of her.

"You know what they say," he offered, fighting the urge to draw her closer.

"There's something about our circumstances people 'say'?"

He smiled softly, the idea gelling in his mind. "There is— If you can't beat them…"

"What are you talking about?"

"Join them," he offered. "Haven't you ever heard that saying?"

"Join them in what?"

"Thinking we're married."

Her eyes narrowed. "That's ridiculous."

"No, it's not. Think about it for a second. What if we were to buy into it along with the rest of them and be married for a while?"

"You're suggesting we pretend we really *are* married?"

"We don't have to pretend," he reminded her.

"You know what I mean."

"We had fun in Vegas. Didn't we have fun in Vegas? You liked me there, right?"

"Vegas was a fantasy."

"But you married me. That means I'm not such a bad guy." He gave in and drew her toward him, letting them glide to a stop on the far side of the pond.

She gazed up at him, and there was a hint of something encouraging in her blue eyes. "You're a liar, a cheat and a con man."

He tipped his head, hoping he was right about the message in her eyes. "But you want to kiss me anyway."

"No, I don't."

"Liar," he whispered, moving closer.

"This better be for show," she said.

"This isn't for show."

"Jack."

"I really am going to kiss you."

"I can't pretend we're married."

"Sure you can." His lips touched hers.

They were cool and soft and erotically delicious. In a split second, she was kissing him back.

He twined their fingers together, deepening the kiss, bending her backward, fighting the instinct to pull her fully into his arms. He kissed her as long as he dared. Then he slowly broke away.

"This is a bad idea," she said.

"This is the best idea I've ever had. We are *great* together."

He could see her skepticism.

He could tell she was about to say no, so he kept on talking. "Plus, we both know it's a fantasy. How can there be anything wrong with a good fantasy?"

"Jack."

"There's some serious chemistry between us, Kristy. I know it, and you sure know it." He could still feel her slick body responding under his hands. "We're both adults," he continued huskily. "We have a fantastic time. And we both walk away at the end."

He kissed her again, this time he kept going until she was breathless.

"Where's the harm?" he asked against her mouth.

She inhaled deeply, hesitated, then spoke. "Can I think about it?"

No! he wanted to shout.

"Sure," he said instead.

"No. Oh, *no!*" Sinclair's shriek echoed in the distance.

Jack and Kristy turned to the sound.

Hunter was behind her, hands on her hips, pushing her faster and faster and faster across the pond.

Jack couldn't help but chuckle.

"She's going to kill him," Kristy muttered.

"I'd say he's got the upper hand."

"Sooner or later, he'll have to stop. And then she'll kill him."

Jack doubted that.

He put an arm around Kristy. He wasn't going to waste valuable time worrying about his cousin. He drew her against his side. It felt good, too good. He wished he dared put forward another argument. He couldn't bear the thought of another celibate night sleeping next to her in his bed. There were moments when he honestly thought it might kill him.

But he knew he had to wait. Married or not, he was asking her for a holiday fling, and she had every right to say no.

Kristy was going to say yes.

She'd known it before breakfast.

Heck, she'd known it half the night.

She'd forced herself to sleep on the idea. But deep down inside, she'd known all along she was going to make love with

Jack again. He and Vegas had been constantly on her mind. It showed in the way her body hummed around him, and it showed in the fantasy clothes she'd created.

She was staring at them now. Megan and Isabella weren't due for another half hour. Every morning, they dropped their kids off at school before making their way to the mansion.

Kristy ran her fingers over the waterfall dress and the hot-air-balloon pants, holding the kicky crop top up against her chest.

She'd added a bikini for the swim she and Jack hadn't taken at the waterfall. She'd also mocked-up a cocktail dress out of a gorgeous piece of hand-dyed Mikado silk. It was black at the bottom, rising to midnight blue and orange then yellow like the desert sunset they'd shared.

She'd also created a sexy wisp of a dress, dark green from the casino, with diamonds of lace inset in the sides. But the crowning finale, the one she couldn't wait to finish, was a dramatic red charmeuse silk evening gown. It was strapless, with a tight bodice and a straight full-length skirt. She'd sewn tiny triangles of lace into the hemline, flouncing it out with crinoline to mimic the roulette wheel.

She sighed.

Maybe someday she'd see one of these on a runway.

"Hey, Kristy?"

Before Kristy could react, Sinclair was through the door and into the workshop.

"There you are," said Sinclair.

Kristy shifted in front of the collection, hoping her sister wouldn't notice it. "I knocked on your door this morning," she told her sister.

"I guess I slept in."

"What happened? Did you two stay up late fighting?"

Kristy and Jack had left Sinclair and Hunter in the great room with mugs of liquor-laced hot chocolate and in the midst of a ridiculous debate about dating etiquette.

"I won pretty quick," Sinclair told her, her gaze sliding to the clothes. "What are those?"

Kristy blocked her view even further. "Just...uh...something I'm fooling around with."

Sinclair went around her.

"They're great," she said with genuine enthusiasm, lifting the green dress on its hanger and holding it against her body. "Very sexy."

"These, over here, are the ones for the show." Kristy tried to direct Sinclair's attention to the Irene collection.

But Sinclair wouldn't be distracted. "You made all of them?" She put the green dress back and switched to the waterfall dress.

"I did," said Kristy. "But, these ones—"

"Are boring," said Sinclair, with a dismissive wave of her hand. "Why not take the good ones to London?"

Kristy raised her eyebrows at the ludicrous suggestion. "I can't."

"Why not?"

"Because I've had expert help with *this* collection. And it's the one Cleveland and I made the deal on."

"So, tell him you've changed your mind."

"I can't change my mind."

Sinclair traded the waterfall dress for the crop top. "Then tell Jack you've changed your mind."

"I can't do that, either."

Jack didn't respect her skills or her talent. He was only going along with having her in the contest because Cleveland had forced him.

"You're sleeping with him, right?"

Kristy didn't know what to say to that.

Sinclair watched her closely, then her voice took on an unnatural calm. "Right, Kristy. Because he *is* your *husband*."

Kristy blinked like a deer in the headlights.

Sinclair plunked the crop top back on the rack. "Damn it," she swore. "I hoped he was lying."

"Huh?"

"Hunter, dear sister." Sinclair paced in a semicircle around Kristy. "Your cousin-in-law told me your marriage was a sham."

Kristy opened her mouth, but nothing came out.

"He said Jack only married you to save his grandfather from a fortune hunter."

Kristy recognized the angry crackle in Sinclair's familiar blue eyes. She'd hated deceiving her sister.

"Am I not your partner in crime?" asked Sinclair.

Kristy struggled to frame a response.

Then a note of real hurt crept into Sinclair's voice. "Why would you lie to me?"

"Because I didn't want *you* to have to lie for *me*."

"To Mom and Dad?"

"Yes!" It was a choice between bad and worse.

"I've been lying to Mom and Dad for you since we were born."

"Not like this."

"What the hell happened?"

"I thought Hunter told you."

"Not all of it." Sinclair took a step forward. "He didn't know why you said yes. Why'd you go and marry Jack?"

Kristy didn't know.

She honestly didn't know.

"There were helicopters," she tried. "And dinner and dancing. Oh, Sinclair, you should see him in a suit."

"You were hot for him? That's it?"

"Totally," Kristy admitted.

Sinclair laughed softly. "I can respect that. But you couldn't have settled for a fling?"

"He proposed."

"The rat bastard," said Sinclair, but there was a wry grin along with the insult.

"As it turned out," said Kristy on a sigh.

"So, now what?"

"Now, I put these away, finish the *real* collection and go to London and try to win that darn contest." Kristy scooped two of the fantasy dresses from the rack and headed for the closet.

"Mistake," said Sinclair, nodding to Kristy's armload. "Those dresses are better. And he owes you."

"Do you have any idea how much they've spent on me already? I'm coming away just fine from this deal."

"Did you sign a prenup?"

"We are *not* going after his money." Kristy transferred the evening gown to the closet.

Sinclair leaned to peer out the window. "That's a whole lot of money, babe."

"And it's his, not mine."

"Depends on the state."

"I signed a prenup."

Sinclair gave a sigh of disgust. "Did I teach you nothing?"

"This is not a scenario even *you* could have contemplated." Kristy all but sprinted to the closet with the remaining items.

"What about future planning?" Sinclair called. "Self-preservation? Keeping your sister in the style to which she's planning to become accustomed?"

Kristy latched the closet. "Don't you have a plane to catch?"

"I could stay through the holidays, eat caviar, sip champagne."

"I thought you said they needed you at work."

"They do."

"And we can't both miss Christmas dinner."

"So you get to stay here with the hunky husband and eat caviar and drink champagne?"

Kristy crossed her arms over her chest in mock censure. "You got your sights set on my hunky husband?"

"Not exactly. But did you get a good look at his cousin?"

"You fought with Hunter all night long."

"Not the entire night."

Kristy stared at her sister's telltale expression. "You didn't," she whispered.

"Got a plane to catch," sang Sinclair, turning for the door.

Kristy hustled after her. "What *happened?*"

"The hot chocolate was great. He was cute. And there was all that leftover adrenaline from skating."

"So you jumped his bones?"

"It was more the other way around."

"I don't believe this." Then a memory kicked in. "Oh, wow. You have red hair."

"Yeah? It's how most people tell us apart."

"Plus, I'm taller."

"A single inch. Get over it."

"You slept with Hunter."

Sinclair responded with a secretive smile.

"Is this in some way going to screw up my life?" asked Kristy.

"Relax," said Sinclair. "We're both grown-ups, and it was a one-time, impetuous thing."

"You're not going to call him?"

"Not in a million years. It wasn't that good."

"It was so."

"Okay, it was. But I'm not going to call him. Quit worrying. Phone me from London. And take the cool clothes!"

"Fallen for your wife yet?" asked Hunter, sauntering into Jack's study in the early afternoon.

For a split second Jack wondered if Hunter had found out about his phone call this morning to Zenia Topaz, and the huge favor he'd just called in. But then he realized his cousin was only fishing.

He pointedly opened a financial report on a beauty products company acquisition that Cleveland was consider-ing. "Don't you have work to do?"

Hunter shrugged, stopping in front of the desk. "I'm on holiday."

"Then how come I'm not?"

"Because you're a workaholic?" Hunter picked up a round, crystal paper weight and tossed it from hand to hand. "Or maybe it's because you're trying to keep your mind off a certain knockout blonde who's making you crazy."

Jack scoffed away the notion. "In case you haven't noticed, that knockout blonde is married to me…and sleeping with me." The last part was only technically true, of course. But Hunter didn't need to know that.

"Back to my original question," said Hunter, "have you fallen for your wife yet?"

Jack glanced back down at the spreadsheet, pushing aside images of Kristy asleep in his bed. "Absolutely not."

Only a fool would fall for his bride of convenience. Naturally, he wanted to make love with her. Who wouldn't? And he wanted her to succeed—as much for Sierra Sanchez as anything. But he was a long way from feeling more than lust, admiration and respect.

"If you're sure," said Hunter.

"I'm sure," said Jack.

Hunter set down the paperweight. "The moms wanted me to remind you about the sleigh ride tonight. Seven sharp."

"I'll remember," Jack assured him.

Hunter moved to the doorway and stood there for a moment. "Mind if Kristy rides with me?"

Jack felt as if he'd been punched in the solar plexus. He glance sharply at his cousin. "Yes." *Hell, yes.* He bit back an order for Hunter to keep away.

A knowing grin grew on Hunter's face. "Gotcha," he exclaimed, backing out before Jack could form a response.

Not that there was any response Jack could reasonably form. Because Hunter was right to laugh at him. He was feeling entirely too possessive of Kristy. He was beginning to act as if she was his real wife. In fact, he was beginning to *wish* she was his real wife.

He turned back to the financial report, forcing the unsettling thought from his mind.

Kristy shoved Sinclair and Hunter, and Sinclair's cavalier advice from her mind for the day. She had more pressing issues, like struggling to perfect the Irene collection and watching the clock until it was time for Isabella and Megan to head home. She couldn't wait to talk to Jack.

Jack.

She smiled just thinking about being held in his arms again. Then she got a hollow feeling in the pit of her stomach when she thought about the holidays ending.

Christmas Day was rushing up on them. And she was leaving the day after that. She'd already filled out a dozen forms for London, and her trunks were being shipped at the end of the week. The collection would be sent on a transport plane to meet up with her at the event. Cleveland had insisted on buying her a first-class ticket, accommodations at the luxury Claymore Diamond Hotel and limo service to and from the airport.

As she closed the last of the cupboards and drawers, she heard bells jingling outside. Then footsteps bounded up the stairs and Jack stuck his head in through the doorway. "You ready?"

"For what?"

"A one-horse open sleigh."

"Really?"

"Well, two horses. We're going along the river trail."

The harness bells jingled louder.

Kristy smiled to herself, forgetting about the end of their relationship, forgetting everything but the night stretching out in front of her. A romantic sleigh ride. What a perfect place to tell Jack she was on board, she wanted to pretend their marriage was real for a while.

"Let me grab my coat," she said.

"I've got gloves and a hat waiting for you downstairs."

Zipping up, she all but bounced down to the driveway where, to her disappointment, she noticed each sleigh held four people.

Cleveland, Aunt Gwen and Melanie were in the front sleigh with Hunter, while Jack and Kristy were riding with his mother and Elaine.

"You're in for a treat," said Elaine as Jack helped her up and over the lip of the sleigh. "The neighbors have a decorating competition every year."

"I can't wait," said Kristy, swallowing her disappointment and pasting a smile on her face. "Hello, Liza."

"I see you've been working hard," Liza responded with formality.

"I have a lot to do," said Kristy.

"I notice the jet's been busy—"

"Mother," said Jack, taking his own seat.

"I'm simply pointing out that Kristy has a fine selection of materials to work with."

"That I do," agreed Kristy, deciding to ignore Liza's jabs. "Thanks to Jack." She patted his thigh as he spread a plaid wool blanket over their laps.

He shot her a look of surprise. She kept her expression neutral as the horses stepped forward and the sleigh jerked to a glide.

Elaine and Liza were facing rear with an identical blanket covering their legs. A top-hatted driver sat up front on a raised seat, while two tawny-colored, golden-maned Clydesdales shook their heads and jingled the bells on their harnesses.

Settled against Jack's warmth, Kristy accepted the delay in her seduction plans and sat back to enjoy the view of the Oslands' gardens as they made their way toward the river trail.

Tiny white lights trimmed the branches of bare oak trees, while swooping ropes of color lined the hedges. Snow-covered spotlights gave the frozen fountains an incandescent glow. And, in the middle of it all, one huge pine tree sparkled color and shine all the way up to a golden star on top.

Kristy rested her head on Jack's shoulder. In response, he stretched his arm across the bench seat behind her.

"I've been thinking about a party," said Liza.

Jack looked at his mother. "I thought we were doing the big Christmas dinner this year."

"I don't mean a Christmas party," she responded. "I mean a wedding party."

Kristy straightened.

"People will expect something," Liza continued. "Perhaps at the Club, after the holidays."

"Mom, I'm not sure that's a good—"

"Nonsense." Liza interrupted. "You cheated Kristy out of a wedding."

"It wasn't him," Kristy put in.

"You told me he talked you into the hotel chapel," said Elaine.

Kristy glanced guiltily at Jack. She had decided to stick to the truth as much as possible. "But I wasn't holding out for a big wedding."

Liza and Elaine waited for her to elaborate.

"It was, uh, more the length of…"

Jack gave her shoulder a squeeze. "She couldn't decide whether to settle for me."

Kristy shot a glance skyward. "Nice, Jack."

"What?"

"You just told your mother I thought you weren't good enough."

Liza's lips pursed.

Elaine started to chuckle. "He's not."

"Yeah, right," said Kristy, with an exaggerated sigh. "Handsome, rich, intelligent and funny. I guess I was holding out for somebody who could also—I don't know—sing opera."

Elaine laughed again, and even Liza smiled.

"I can sing," insisted Jack.

"And that's what clinched it, darling," Kristy purred.

"Back to the party," said Liza. But she seemed more relaxed now.

"Look," Jack called, pointing across the river to a resplendent Santa display. The lighted reindeer swooped through the air. Santa's sleigh was festooned with red and green and white lights. The jolly old man himself glowed with tiny red lights that outlined his suit and his sack full of toys. In the background was a lighted Christmas forest—each tree glowing its very own color.

"Nice," said Kristy. "Times Square has nothing on you guys."

"It's most definitely a competition," said Jack. "As far back as I can remember, the Smythes tried to outdo the Comptons who tried to outdo the Baileys and so on."

"Has your family always spent Christmas here?" Kristy asked everyone in general, hoping to keep talk away from anything wedding-related.

"Since we were kids," answered Elaine.

"Hunter's family, too," Jack said.

The horses made their way past discrete pot lights lining the pathway, moving toward the faint glow of the next property.

"How does your family celebrate, Kristy?" asked Liza.

"Our Christmases were nothing like this," Kristy answered. "We had a house in Brooklyn. Nice neighborhood, plenty of decorations, even carolers—"

Jack took her hand in his beneath the blanket. His gaze caught hers, his eyes darker than usual, the muffled sound of the horses' hooves and the muted snatches of voices from the other sleigh filled the sharp, sweet air.

A rich, steady burn started in the center of her body. It radiated out, fingers of heat licking at her skin. She wanted to tell him she was in. She wanted to tell him so, for now and for later, for as many days as they had left. They could laugh, kiss, make love and sleep in each others' arms.

Another resplendent estate came into view.

Liza and Elaine craned their necks.

Unable to wait any longer, Kristy stretched up to whisper in Jack's ear. "Yes."

He jerked back, staring down at her with wide eyes.

She gave him a nod and a secretive smile.

He squeezed her hand. Then he pulled her close, the warmth of his body seeping deeply into hers.

Ten

Kristy barely remembered the rest of the sleigh ride, and dinner had taken forever. Their gazes had practically melted each other over crème brûlée and cognac. But if anybody noticed, they were too polite to say.

They were also too polite to make a comment when Jack declared bedtime at nine-twenty-seven.

Kristy forced herself to say a measured good-night, happy that Liza seemed to be starting to like her, and that she'd agreed to postpone talk of a wedding party until after the New Year. Elaine's eyes twinkled when they met Kristy's, but Kristy couldn't bring herself to care. She was too busy struggling to keep from sprinting up the stairs.

The second the bedroom door was shut behind them, Jack pulled her into his arms. His openmouthed kiss was instantaneous. She answered in kind as his fingers fumbled with the buttons of her blouse.

She pushed his suit jacket off his shoulders, frantically working on his shirt as they gasped and kissed then kissed again. She yanked her arms out of the blouse, letting it drop to the floor. He snapped off her bra, then cradled her face with his palms, kissing her over and over and over.

When he finally drew back, it was to rip off his shirt. Then he shucked his pants and fisted his hands in the fabric of her skirt, pulling it higher and higher, revealing her white silk panties, then slipping his thumbs beneath the delicate elastic.

She spread her palms across his broad chest, reveling in the texture of his muscles, stroking up to his shoulders, then down again, further and further, until he gasped and his hands gripped her buttocks.

"Don't," he pleaded.

"Why not?" She wanted him, wanted him right here, right now, right this instant.

In answer, he scooped her into his arms and deposited her on the bed. Then he pushed her skirt up to her waist and stripped off her panties in one swift motion.

"Too fast for you?" he rasped.

"Not fast enough." While he watched, gaze burning hot, she let her thighs drift apart, her feet dangle off the edge of the high mattress. She slowly, sensually raked spread fingers through her hair, loosening the ponytail, then dropped her hands to rest beside her head.

Jack squeezed his eyes shut and groaned.

He joined her on the bed, his palm covering her mound, his fingers sliding slickly and surely inside.

She arched her hips. "Yes."

He kissed her shoulder, her neck, her breast, increasing his rhythm as he drew a beaded nipple into his mouth.

"Now," she begged. "Please, now."

"Not yet," he rumbled, slowing down, feathering more kisses along her sensitive skin, whispering erotic promises in her ear.

She writhed against him, her hands grasping sections of the downy quilt.

His mouth moved to hers. He shifted across her, one thigh replacing the hand that was driving her insane. She welcomed his weight, wrapped her arm around him, stroked her palms down his back, lower to his buttocks, pulling him to her, urging him inside.

He paused to gaze into her eyes. They hovered there, frozen for a heartbeat.

"Kristy," he breathed.

Then he pressed surely and swiftly into her, and her world turned to a kaleidoscope of sensations.

She brought her legs around his waist, and her arms around his neck, plastering her body against his, smelling his musk, tasting the salt of his skin, hearing the rasp of his labored breathing and feeling, oh, yes, feeling the slick heat of his body as he moved endlessly with hers on a plane above paradise.

He held her there. Held her, held her, held her until her body wanted to scream for mercy. Every nerve ending tingled. Every pore opened wide. Every ounce of hormone and passion her body possessed gathered and crested and hung suspended in space and time.

Then he cried her name again, and the dam burst free. Convulsions of color galloped through her mind over and over again.

Moments later, her muscles gave out. She all but melted into the mattress, Jack's body a delicious weight pressing her into the soft oblivion.

"You okay?" came his hoarse voice.

"Yes." She tried to nod, but something got lost in the message from her brain. She couldn't move an inch.

"Seriously," he said.

"Seriously," she assured him.

He took a couple more deep, shuddering breaths. "I didn't remember *that*," he rumbled.

"I remember something," she said, her strength slowly returning. "But I didn't remember a super nova and angels singing. Do you suppose we're dead?"

He chuckled, his entire body shaking in reaction. "If this is dead, I can handle it."

"Yeah. Me, too," she sighed.

He shifted his weight from her, holding her securely in his arms. "But I hope it's not."

"I'd hate to miss London."

They were both silent for a moment, and his fingertips toyed with a lock of her hair.

"How's that going?" he asked.

Kristy felt a twinge of unease. "I really appreciate everything you've bought me. Really I do."

"But…"

"It's hard."

They were both silent again, and she turned her head so that she could look at him. "It's really hard."

"Can I help?"

She shook her head. "You've done so much already."

"I want to help," he said.

"It's nothing you can find or buy. It's the clothes, the designs." How could she explain?

"You don't think they're good enough?"

"I don't know what to think."

Jack wrapped her in a big hug. "It's going to be okay."

She could feel a tear at the corner of her eye. "What if it's not? I've spent all your money—"

"You haven't spent all my money. You couldn't begin to spend all my money."

He kissed her forehead. "It'll be better in the morning."

"How?" She'd still have two collections. She'd still be confused and pulled in opposite directions.

"I'm not sure." He sounded a bit sad. "But it will be. It always is."

Kristy wanted to argue, but there was no point. Despite Sinclair's optimism, Kristy feared the clothes that made her happy would never sell. And the clothes that would sell would never make her happy.

At the end of another long sewing day, Kristy made her way from the workshop to the house. Lights lined the curving driveway, delineated the porch and the roof line, and dotted every tree and shrub within a hundred yards of the main staircase.

Snowflakes floated down from the dark sky, settling on the naked oak tree branches, blurring the points of colored light and adding to the magic of the front garden.

Suddenly, she saw Jack.

He'd been waiting for her, sitting on the steps in his beautiful black wool coat and black leather gloves.

"Hey," she said, mustering some enthusiasm into her voice. She shouldn't have confessed her fears last night. The last thing she wanted was for Jack to think she couldn't pull off a collection for the contest.

"Hey, yourself," he stood and trotted down the stairs to meet her.

His dark hair was perfectly combed, face freshly shaven. It wasn't an unusual look for him, but she didn't remember there being a Christmas event tonight.

"I have a surprise for you," he said, taking her arm to guide her up the stairs.

Kristy resisted. "What kind of a surprise?"

"I need you to go upstairs and get dressed."

"Are we going somewhere?"

"We're staying in."

"Just you and me?" If so, why did she need to dress up? They'd be naked pretty soon if the look in his eyes was anything to go by.

"And a few others," he said. "It's a dinner party." He held her hand. "Come on."

This time, she followed him up the stairs, through the door, into the foyer that was festooned with pine garland, holly wreaths and white tapered candles.

"Why all the secrecy?" she asked as they headed up the main staircase.

"Because that's how you do a surprise."

"I feel silly."

"Well, you're about to feel great. Because that's what all the best surprises do for you." He paused at his bedroom door. "And *I* do really good surprises."

She couldn't help but smile at his self-confidence.

"To start," he said, pushing open the door. "A dress."

Kristy stopped to admire the lovely black silk dress with red spaghetti straps and piping, and a chiffon overskirt.

"It's a Zenia Topaz," he said.

"I know," said Kristy, moving forward. "I love her work."

"Good. Now, put it on."

Kristy took a quick shower, refreshed her makeup, brushed her hair, and slipped into the silky-soft creation. It fitted perfectly.

"How did you do this?" she whispered to Jack, turning so he could fasten the buttons.

"It was easy." His hands were warm against her skin, and he kissed the tip of her shoulder when he was done.

Then he reached around her, holding a long aqua box in front of her eyes.

"This goes with it," he said softly.

"I can't," she shook her head, recognizing the big, white bow that was Tiffany's signature.

"Ahh, but you must." He pulled the end of the bow.

She watched, mesmerized, as the ribbon fell away and he reached around with his other hand to open the box.

"It goes with the dress," he said, revealing a delicate choker of large, square-cut rubies.

"Jack," she breathed in astonishment. He made it so hard for her to remember reality.

"You'll be glad you did," he said, removing the necklace from the box. "Trust me on this." He fastened it around her neck.

She knew she should refuse, but she had a feeling it would be futile. Then, she turned to look in the mirror, and she no longer wanted to refuse. The necklace was stunning against her throat.

"Shall we go to dinner?" he gently asked.

She took a very deep breath, sliding into the fantasy. She was Mrs. Osland for tonight, and for tomorrow night and for three more nights after that.

"It's beautiful," she said to Jack.

"You're what's beautiful," he replied, taking her hand and twining her fingers with his.

She entered the dining room on Jack's arm.

It was set with white linen and sterling silver, with three holly-and-white-candle centerpieces flickering in a line down the middle of the long table.

Cleveland sat at one end, with Liza presiding at the other. Elaine, Hunter, Melanie and Aunt Gwen were also present, along with a diminutive woman whom Kristy vaguely recognized. In her mid-forties, the woman had short, dark hair and a narrow face. Her eyes were a beautiful, deep brown. She was also wearing a—

Kristy nearly staggered to a stop.

Zenia Topaz.

Zenia Topaz was sitting at Jack's dining-room table.

Hunter rose from his chair next to her.

"Zenia," said Jack. "I'd like you to meet Kristy Mahoney. My wife."

Kristy found her voice. "Ms. Topaz, it's an honor—"

"Zenia, please," the woman's laughter tinkled. "The dress looks wonderful on you."

Kristy glanced down. "Did you bring the dress?"

Zenia nodded. "I hope Jack wasn't lying when he said you'd like it."

"No." Kristy shook her head. "I love it. And I'm so happy to meet you."

She couldn't believe she was talking to Zenia Topaz.

Hunter moved to one side and gestured to the chair he'd been occupying. "Please, Kristy. Sit."

She glanced at Jack.

"You're the guest of honor," he said.

"Zenia's the guest of honor." Kristy accepted Hunter's offer and smiling a greeting at the others around the table, she sat.

"Red or white, ma'am?" asked one of the stewards.

"Red, thank you," said Kristy as Jack and Hunter took their own seats.

"Jack tells me you're entering Matte Fashion," Zenia said to Kristy.

Other conversations started around the table and blended into the background as the staff served a crab salad appetizer.

"I've been working on a collection," Kristy answered.

"Would you mind if I took a look at it?"

Kristy hesitated, but quickly caught herself. "Of course not."

Zenia's dark eyes turned kind. "I understand you're experiencing some frustrations."

Kristy's stomach bottomed out. "Jack told you that?"

"It's why he asked me to come."

Kristy glanced at her husband, not sure whether to be grateful or offended. "He wants you to help me?"

"He thought a professional eye couldn't hurt."

Kristy nodded. It was true, of course. Kind of hard on the ego, but then she was the one who'd expressed her doubts to him.

Then, an idea took root in Kristy's mind. She could show Zenia the fantasy collection. If Zenia liked it, Kristy would have an ally. And there was a chance, a good chance, that Zenia could sway Jack.

Kristy felt a surge of hope.

She couldn't wait to finish dinner and get out to the workshop.

Kristy started with Irene's collection.

"Very nice," said Zenia with a nod, closely examining the last piece.

Dinner over, she and Kristy were alone in the workshop.

"It has extremely strong technical merit," Zenia continued, motioning to the pieces set up on mannequins. "I like the lines. You were wise to stick to the classics. I particularly like the tailoring on the blouse, and the sleeve detail definitely lifts it from the ordinary."

Kristy tried to pay attention to the analysis, but her mind was galloping ahead to Zenia's reaction to the fantasy collection.

"You might want to rework the bathing suit," said Zenia, moving to look at it. "It's fun, but it's out of step with the other pieces. Have you thought about a single color instead of a print?"

Kristy nodded. But her gaze strayed to the furthest closet.

"You could go with two contrasting colors." Zenia pointed to a blue square on the geometric pattern. Then she pointed to a red line. Red on top, blue on the bottom?"

"Sure."

Zenia peered at her. "Is everything okay?"

Kristy nodded.

"You seem distracted."

Kristy swallowed, and her heart rate increased. She told herself it was now or never. "There's something—" Her voice rasped over her dry throat. "Would you mind looking at something else?"

"Not at all."

Kristy walked to the closet, forcing herself to measure her steps, her heartbeat deep and thick inside her chest. Sweat was breaking out on her palms. She opened the door and retrieved the waterfall dress.

"They're something…" she said to Zenia as she carried it across the room "…something I've been, you know," she laughed nervously, "just playing around with." She hung the dress on a rack then went back for the next piece.

Zenia cocked her head as the collection grew.

Once Kristy had all the pieces out, Zenia walked around the rack with a piercing stare.

After a full minute's silence, Zenia finally spoke. "I think," she said, and then she paused.

Kristy held her breath.

"It's a risk," said Zenia. "For a new designer."

"Can I take a risk?" asked Kristy.

What was the difference between risk and imagination? How did you get the sparkle without taking a risk? Why were all these people telling her to get creative and then advising her to stick with the standard?

Zenia paused again, clearly searching for words. "Later in your career, perhaps. Especially if you establish yourself in Europe and you're looking for a high-end niche. But you're probably not going to find really broad appeal in the domestic market with this."

Kristy nodded, biting her tongue against the arguments that formed in her heart.

"Have I disappointed you?"

Kristy shook her head, then she stopped. "Maybe just a little."

"It's a tough business."

"I'm definitely learning that."

"You have to be flexible starting out. And it helps to have the hide of a rhino."

Kristy tried to smile at the joke. But she was tired of being flexible, tired of taking other people's advice. She knew how Jack felt about experts but, honestly, she wished somebody would give her a smidgen of credit occasionally.

"You have a solid start here," said Zenia, turning back to the Irene collection. "Win or lose, take advantage of the Breakout Designer Contest to start establishing yourself. I'll be there cheering for you. And I know you have a huge supporter in Jack."

"Jack's been amazing," Kristy agreed.

She knew now it was Zenia who'd chosen the fabric and accessories that had arrived in a steady stream from Europe. She knew now that Zenia and Jack were friends, and that Jack had enlisted Zenia's aid.

She should be more grateful.

She owed it to Jack to be a lot more grateful.

Eleven

Jack stroked his fingertip along the curve of Kristy's shoulder, simply because he liked touching her skin.

"You're quiet tonight," he said softly, inhaling the scent of her hair, enjoying the feel of her naked body against his in the afterglow of their lovemaking.

"I guess I've been working hard," she responded.

There were only two days left before they said their final goodbyes and she flew to London for the contest. They'd have Christmas Eve and Christmas Day together—that was all. She was flying out on the twenty-sixth, and he was purposely ignoring the meaning of that moment.

"Jack?" She turned onto her back, staring up at him, her cheeks flushed. She looked very serious. "Can I ask you something?"

Did he dare hope? Would she broach the future? Because he'd been thinking about their future a whole lot lately. He hoped they had one.

"It's about the contest."

Not quite what he'd been expecting. But, okay.

He nodded.

She sat up, wrapping the sheet around her naked breasts. "I have these ideas."

He waited.

She laughed nervously. "Well, really, they're…" She stopped talking.

"Yes?"

She bit her bottom lip. "I made some clothes."

"I know," he said slowly.

She frowned. "I made some other clothes."

He struggled to understand her point.

She reached out and touched his forearm. "I had some ideas that were different than Irene's. So I made them. And I like them. And I want to show them in London."

"Where in London?" He could probably help.

"At the contest."

"At Matte Fashion?"

She gave a rapid nod.

"But you already have a collection for Matte Fashion."

"I want to show a different one."

Jack didn't know what to say. It was only forty-eight hours before she'd be in London. "Irene helped you with this one. Zenia helped you, too."

"Hear me out."

He cocked his head sideways, biting back the obvious arguments.

"I think mine—the other outfits—are better. I really do. Everybody keeps asking me for sparkle. I think these have sparkle."

This was crazy. "Has anyone seen them besides you? Has Cleveland?"

"Zenia saw them."

"And, did she like them?"

"She wasn't really clear. She said they were a risk."

Jack sighed. "Kristy, I think *risk* is a euphemism for 'weak'."

"Not necessarily."

"Kristy—"

"Not necessarily, Jack. What if they're a good risk? I feel…" She pressed her palm against her chest. "In here, Jack. I can't explain it, but I fell like I *know*. You know?"

Jack had to nip this in the bud. He couldn't let Kristy go out there and embarrass herself. And he sure wouldn't let her compromise Sierra Sanchez.

"I was paying her to be here," he said. "She knew you were my wife. So of course she's going to be polite."

Kristy squared her bare shoulders. "So, you don't believe in me."

"Of *course* I believe in you."

"No. You believe in yourself. If you truly believed in me, you'd take a chance. You can't always do the safe thing, Jack."

The safe thing? Jack came into a sitting position. "When have I ever done the safe thing around you?"

"Marrying me wasn't mitigating risk?"

"You know what I thought back then."

"Yes, I do know what you thought," she said. "And you were mitigating the risk to your family."

Okay, he'd agree with that. Not that it was a crime.

"And you've been mitigating it ever since."

Now *that* he could not agree with. "I haven't been doing anything ever since."

She held out one arm expansively. "You bought me the finest materials, the finest equipment, the finest advice and assistance."

"And this is a problem, why?"

"Because you practically hired a babysitter in Zenia. You built me a safety net ten miles wide."

"That's what you do when the stakes are high. You play it safe." He was making good business decisions, simple as that.

"No, that's not what you do when the stakes are high."

"And this is based on your years of experience dealing in high stakes?"

She sat back, compressing her lips. "There's no need to get insulting."

"I'm not—"

"You hired me to do a job," she tersely reminded him. "It would be nice if you'd let me do it."

"We *did* let you do it." The woman had been sewing for three weeks straight.

"No, you didn't. You were so busy circling the wagons—"

"That's ridiculous."

"No…" Her voice trailed away, and a faraway look came into her eyes. "In fact, it's all been pretty insulting."

His spine stiffened. "So sorry to have *insulted* you."

She gave a chopped laugh. "You know, now that I think about it, I was so busy convincing myself to be grateful, that I didn't even see you were smothering me."

Oh, so now he was smothering her? "Did you happen to *see* that I was spending a fortune? Or did you happen to *see* that you were consuming a fortune?"

She clamped her mouth shut.

He figured he'd made his point. But then her eyes turned to green fire, and he realized how harsh their words had become. They were practically yelling at each other.

He didn't want that.

He didn't want to fight with her, and he didn't want to hurt her. All he wanted was for her to be happy.

"Can we please stop?" he asked.

The fight seemed to go out of her, and her voice dropped to a whisper. "No. I don't think we can."

"I don't want to fight with you, Kristy."

"You simply want to do things your way?"

Well, yeah. That was basically what he had in mind.

His expression must have said as much because she shrank back.

"Kristy." He reached for her, but she was too fast.

She was off the bed, dragging the sheet with her. "I need to go," she choked out.

"We can talk about this."

"Talk about what? We can't talk about my career. Shall we talk about how you want to sleep with me, but it's only temporary?"

He opened his mouth to protest, but she kept talking.

"I thought it wouldn't matter, Jack. I thought I could take your money and your great sex, and whatever crumbs of respect you threw my way."

Crumbs? *Crumbs?* He'd given her everything that was in his power to give.

"But, I can't," she said. "I just—"

"Fine," he cut her off, his instincts turning to self-protection. "If you want it to end, by all means, pick a guest room. You've done your duty and then some."

He looked away, clenching his fists, ordering himself not to beg her to stay.

It was four in the morning on Christmas Day when Kristy finished packing the shipping trunks. She needed some kind of closure, and the simple work also kept her from trudging back to the lonely guest room.

She took one last, long look at her waterfall dress, the hot-air-balloon pants, the sunset and casino dresses, the bikini and the roulette evening gown. With a lump in her throat, she closed the trunk, leaving it with the boxes Isabella had agreed to ship to her in New York after the holidays. The other collection would come with her.

She told herself the Irene collection would be fine. It was a strong entry and a really great step for a young designer like her. She could make some connections at the show, build on the technical merit Zenia had seen in the collection, maybe get a chance to do something more creative in the future. Maybe she could even show the desert collection.

She'd see Zenia in London at the show, and Cleveland

would fly over to represent Sierra Sanchez. But, after today, Kristy would likely never see Jack again.

She told herself it was for the best. What they'd had together wasn't real. It had never been real. It had started on a lie and gone downhill from there.

She latched the last trunk, shrugged into her coat, then wandered down the stairs and outside to the spectacular, twinkling gardens and the softly sprinkling snow. It was turning into a picture-perfect Christmas Day.

Her boots crunched on the driveway as she passed lighted trees, sweeping arches and the meticulously decorated porch and pillars that flanked the double doors. A wreath of boughs and pine cones hung on each one, encircling the polished brass knockers.

Kristy carefully pressed on the left-hand door. The hinges glided open, revealing the festooned, marble entryway. All was still and silent. It was as if the entire house held its breath waiting for Christmas Day to burst upon it.

Even though she was feeling tired and melancholy, Kristy couldn't resist a peek into the great room. A fifteen-foot tree overwhelmed one corner. A huge array of brightly decorated presents stretched halfway into the room, all but burying the stone fireplace. The tree lights were still on, and Kristy smelled fragrant smoke.

Her attention moved to a wisp of white curling into the air from a leather wing chair. It was Hunter.

"Hey," he greeted quietly.

"Hey," she responded, moving to the opposite chair. She had to pick her way around a couple of gifts to get there.

"You're still up?" he asked, swirling a measure of deep amber cognac in a blown crystal snifter. The cognac bottle and a tray with three other glasses sat on the low table between the chairs.

"I was in the workshop." She plunked down.

He held up the cigar. "You mind?"

Kristy shook her head.

Hunter leaned forward and poured a measure of the cognac into a new glass, handing it to Kristy. The fire crackled, and sparks flew off the wood, pinging against the glass front.

"Your last full day," he said.

"It is," Kristy agreed.

He raised his glass in a silent toast, watching her expression carefully.

"Merry Christmas, Kristy Mahoney."

She followed suit. "Merry Christmas to you, Hunter Osland." She took a sip of the expensive cognac.

He considered her over the rim of his glass. "You moved out of his room."

"It was time for me to go."

"But you moved out early."

She shrugged.

"Why?"

She shrugged again.

"Are you in love with him?"

Kristy nearly dropped the glass. "No."

She wasn't in love with Jack. He had simply shown his true colors—absolute allegiance to his corporation, his family and his precious experts.

"You married him," said Hunter.

"That was infatuation. Nobody falls in love in a weekend." She knew that. She'd always known that. She'd just forgotten it for a little while.

"I guess not. I am sorry you got hurt."

"I'm not hurt," she lied.

They both stared silently at the fire.

"What about you?" Kristy finally asked.

"Nothing hurts me."

"You ever been in love?"

He shook his head.

Kristy couldn't help but smile to herself. "Not even with the redheaded girl?"

"Not even with her."

"You know, Sinclair is a redhead."

He turned to Kristy. "Sinclair has a big mouth. And it's auburn."

"So you've noticed."

"I also noticed she's bossy and judgmental."

"Well, if you're going to get picky about it." A slow smile grew on Kristy's face. It felt like the first time she'd smiled in days.

Hunter frowned in return and polished off the cognac.

"We have twin uncles," Kristy noted.

"Kristy."

"I'm just saying, from a gypsy perspective…"

"Go to bed."

She rose and set down her snifter. "And, of course, there's Sinclair and me."

Hunter did a double take. "What?"

"Sinclair and I are twins."

"No, you're not."

"I'm pretty sure we are."

"You're taller."

"We're not identical."

He stared at her for a moment. "Really?"

Kristy leaned into him, stretching her smile from ear to ear. After the past couple of days, it felt good to goof around with somebody. "So, you see, Hunter, it's fate."

A wolfish grin grew on Hunter's face. "Maybe the gypsy didn't mean a redhead with twins. Maybe I get twin redheads. You could dye your hair."

"No, she couldn't," came Jack's deep, censorious voice.

Kristy reflexively jumped back.

"We're just messing around," said Hunter.

"So, I see," Jack growled, glaring at his cousin.

"Don't do this." Kristy scoffed.

He paced into the room. "Don't do what? Interrupt your late-night chat?"

"You know it's nothing."

"I do?"

Hunter came to his feet. "It's nothing, Jack. Trust her, don't trust her. But trust me. It's nothing."

Jack stared at Hunter as the silence thickened.

"Guess I'll head upstairs," Hunter finally offered.

"Good idea," said Jack, shifting his gaze to Kristy.

"I'll come with you," said Kristy.

"I'd like to talk to you," said Jack.

"It's late."

"No kidding."

She heaved a sigh. "I'm tired, and I really don't want to fight with you."

"Who said anything about fighting?"

"Maybe it's that frown on your face."

Jack spared another glance for his cousin. "Good night, Hunter."

"Right," Hunter muttered, heading for the door.

Kristy crossed her arms protectively over her chest, steeling herself against the familiar pulse of desire, promising to end the conversation quickly so she could climb into bed and bury her head under the covers.

Hunter's footfalls disappeared, and the silence seemed to boom off the walls. Firelight flickered on Jack's hard profile, shimmering in his hair, sparking the depths of his slate gray eyes.

He reached for the cognac bottle and poured himself a drink.

"You said you wanted to talk?" she prompted.

He straightened and drew a deep breath. "I really need you to understand."

"Oh, I do understand," she said.

It wasn't so tough to figure out. She was a distant second to Osland International. Understandable, even logical, but hurtful all the same.

He swirled the cognac in the depths of his glass, watching the amber liquid. "It should have been so simple," he sighed.

"Simple?"

He looked up. "I thought we'd be divorced by now. I thought you'd… I expected…"

She put an edge to her voice. "I'm sorry I disappointed you."

He took a step closer. "That's not my point."

"What is your point?"

"My point…" He gazed into her eyes, searching. "Do you have any idea how much I want you right now?"

Kristy's stomach hollowed, while her chest tightened with undeniable desire. "That's an interesting point," she managed.

"You know what I mean."

"It's over, Jack."

"Really? Because it doesn't feel over."

It had to be over. She'd found the strength to walk away last night, and she had to stay away, no matter what.

"Sleep with me tonight," he rasped. "We don't have to make love—"

"I can't." Her voice caught, emotions raw in her chest. It would kill her to sleep with him one more time. And, if it didn't, it would kill her to walk away again.

His voice went thick with emotion. "We had something, Kristy."

No they didn't, they couldn't.

"This week," he continued. "Last week. Back there in Vegas, we seriously had something."

"What we had, Jack, started with a lie, and then we lived another lie. You wanted to save your grandfather, and I wanted to win a contest. We used each other. I'm not very proud of that, are you?"

"I'm not proud," he said. "I'm a lot of things at the moment, but proud isn't one of them." The defeat in his voice leeched the fight right out of her.

"I'm just tired," she confessed.

Compassion turned his eyes to pewter.

He nodded and polished off the drink.

Then he set the glass down on the table. "And you need to go to bed. So, let me just say…" He drew a deep breath. "Goodbye, Kristy."

She gave him a shaky nod, fighting an instinct that urged her to throw herself into his arms, hang on tight and to never let go. Her throat clogged. She could barely get the words out. "Goodbye, Jack."

They stared at each other for a frozen moment. But then he glanced away, focusing on the fire behind her, and it was well and truly over.

Twelve

Three days into the London trip, and Kristy could still see the haunted expression on Jack's face.

"Twelve pounds, ma'am," said the cabdriver, rousing her from her daydream. She realized they'd arrived at the Claymore Diamond Hotel.

She handed the man the fare and what she hoped was an appropriate tip and hopped out of the traditional black car.

Then she stared at the stone facade of the hotel, its lights already burning bright under the gloomy afternoon sky. She'd wandered aimlessly through a couple of museums, burning up time. This afternoon was the dress rehearsal in the convention center connected to the hotel. Tomorrow night was the big event.

She knew she should be feeling some sense of anticipation, certainly the other contestants she'd met were getting more nervous by the hour. But, she still hadn't emotionally engaged in the Irene collection. And, besides, she couldn't seem to get her thoughts off Jack.

Was he still in Vermont? At the mansion with Cleveland and Dee Dee? Had he flown back to L.A., or to New York?

Did he miss her? Did he think about her? Had he figured out what was between them?

Because she hadn't. And, worst of all, would she regret not sharing her last night with him in his bed after all?

Jack was getting into the limo to head for the airport, when Hunter's bellow stopped him in his tracks.

"You'd better get your butt up here," Hunter called from one of the workshop windows.

"I'll only be a minute," Jack told the uniformed driver.

"Take your time, sir."

"Can you call Simon and give him an update?"

"Yes, sir." The limo driver reached for his cell phone.

Jack slammed the car door then took the workshop stairs two at a time.

"What the hell?" he asked as he walked through the workshop door. "I'm going to miss my meeting in New York."

Hunter gestured to an open trunk of colorful clothes. "Take a look."

Jack stopped short. "Dresses? You called me up here to see dresses?"

"*Kristy's* dresses."

"So, send them to her." Jack was trying desperately not to think about Kristy.

"Not to wear," sneered Hunter. "Do you know what these are?"

Jack knew full well what they were. "Zenia didn't like them," he said.

"And?"

"And nothing. Cleveland made a deal on one set of designs. Irene helped her fix them. Zenia said they were technically strong. While these, these—"

"Are her heart and soul," said Hunter.

Jack flinched.

"She asked you," said Hunter. "She *asked* you."

"Is that what you were cozying up to her about on Christmas Eve?"

Hunter glared daggers. "That's what *her sister* told me."

"Oh."

"Yeah. Oh."

Jack squared his shoulders. "Fine. Is this conversation over?"

"Take the clothes to London," said Hunter.

Jack snorted his disbelief. Like he could drop everything and do that. Like he could compromise Sierra Sanchez's reputation.

"That's something Gramps would do," he said to Hunter.

Hunter took a step forward. "So what?"

"So, I'm not Gramps."

"Maybe not. But, cousin, you need to ask yourself some very serious questions."

Jack turned and started to walk away. He was done here.

"Do you want respect for your business?" called Hunter. "Or do you want Kristy?"

Jack kept walking.

"Do you want more fashion sales? Or do you want Kristy?"

Jack paused at the door, bracing a hand on the jamb.

"Do you want the family fortune? Or do you want Kristy?"

Kristy. There wasn't a doubt in Jack's mind. But how could he give in on every front just to make her happy?

"What if they're good?" Hunter asked softly. "What if *she's* good? What if she's *great* and you took that chance away from her?"

Jack scrambled to weigh the facts. Irene said she was competent. Zenia said the dresses were risky. Everything inside Jack screamed at him to listen to the experts. He always listened to experts. They had the facts, knew the odds, were always right.

"Stop it!" shouted Hunter.

"What?"

"Stop talking yourself out of it."

"I can't."

"Well then here's one for you. What if she loves you?"

Jack faced his cousin.

"She married you," said Hunter. "Somehow Kristy doesn't strike me as the kind of woman who does that lightly. What if she fell in love with you that weekend in Vegas? What if, against all odds, with all the crap you've pulled, she's still in love with you? What do your experts say about that?"

"Who are the experts in love?" Jack all but yelled. "The gypsies?"

"I'd like to think," came Cleveland's level voice from the doorway. "That *I'm* the expert in matters of love."

Jack turned.

With Dee Dee tucked predictably under his arm, Gramps advanced into the room. "You boys both know I've been married a number of times."

"Yeah, Gramps," said Hunter, calmly. "We know."

"And I bet you're wondering how I feel when the young lady and I part ways."

Jack had never once wondered that.

"I feel great," said Cleveland. "There are never any hard feelings. No tears. Everyone has a good time. I never give her another thought."

He walked past Jack and peered into the open trunk. "They're fancy. I'll give her that."

Then he straightened and stood toe-to-toe with Jack, looking his square in the eye. "How 'bout you, boy. You given Kristy another thought since she left?"

Jack didn't answer. He'd done nothing *but* think about Kristy since the moment she'd left the mansion.

"If not," said Cleveland. "Then you both got what you wanted." He glanced at the trunk again. "Sort of. But if you're thinking about her. If missing her is gnawing at your guts, and if you'd give anything to hear her voice or hold her in your arms again. Well, then you've got a problem. Because you're in love, and you've just screwed yourself out of the woman of your dreams."

Cleveland looked down at Dee Dee, ruffling the little dog's head. "Isn't that right, Pookie? Uncle Jack blew it with your mama."

Something that felt like an iceberg slid into Jack's chest and parked itself next to his heart. He stared at Hunter, and Hunter stared back.

"It's noon," said Hunter. "Do the math. You can make it if Simon fuels up now."

Not giving himself another moment to hesitate, Jack grabbed his cell phone, hitting the speed dial for Simon.

"Yes, sir?" came Simon's voice.

"Refile the flight plan. We're going to London."

"Will do. Do you have an ETA for the airport?"

"Twenty minutes."

"Roger that."

Jack flipped his phone shut.

Hunter snapped the catches on the trunk. "Grab an end."

With Kristy's trunk safely on a delivery truck at Heathrow, Hunter taking care of business back in New York and Zenia on deck for the switch off at tonight's fashion event, Jack climbed into the back of the waiting Rolls.

"The Claymore Diamond Hotel, please."

The driver nodded his acknowledgment and closed the door behind Jack.

Jack knew he should try to rest to combat the jet lag, but he was too excited at the possibility of seeing Kristy again.

Could Hunter be right? Was there a chance she was in love with him? If she was, she could make any damn fashion collection she wanted. He'd pay for it. Hell, he'd pay people to wear it if that's what it took to make her happy.

But first, he had to convince her to give him a chance. And that meant starting from scratch, doing it right this time.

He callèd out to the driver. "Excuse me?"

The man glanced in the rearview mirror. "Yes, sir?"

"Can we make a stop at Tiffany's?"

"Very good, sir."

"Thanks." Jack nodded. Hopefully, a two-carat, flawless solitaire engagement ring would start things off on a new, positive note.

"Don't worry about the necklace," said Zenia. "They need you out front right away."

Kristy glanced around at the frantic buzz of the dressing rooms ten minutes before the Breakout Designer Contest. Elbow to elbow, makeup artists and hairdressers put the final touches on the models, seamstresses took care of last-minute repairs, and the technical staff shouted instructions or talked into their headsets. Photographers made their way between the rows of onlookers, searching for that potential cover shot. The lighting technicians were ready, music had been cued and the announcer was flipping through his notes, confirming last-minute changes to the program.

The show's stage manager negotiated a path through the chaos. "Contestants in their seats, please. The news networks will want footage."

Zenia gave Kristy a quick hug. Then she stood back and squeezed her cool hands. "You look fantastic."

"Thanks," Kristy whispered.

She'd designed the dress herself. It was the one thing she'd brought to London with her from the desert collection, short and basic black, with small triangles of lace sewn into the hem and neck, and sleeves capped with lace that matched her waterfall dress.

Early this morning, she'd come to terms with her Irene collection. It was technically sound. Zenia had said so herself. And Kristy could build on that. She could take the creativity part slowly, learn to add the sparkle and imagination as she went along. Zenia had suggested the hide of a rhino. Kristy could be a rhino. A rhino brimming with imagination and passion, but stubborn and driven and willing to take on the world. However hard she had to work, whatever it took, she was going after her dream.

The Breakout Designer Contest was televised because viewers liked to see the expressions on the contestant's faces when their fashions were paraded across the catwalk. They particularly liked to see the delight on the winner's face at the end of the evening.

So, along with her eleven fellow contestants, Kristy left the backstage area, took the small, side staircase down to the floor, and slid into her seat in the front row.

A program was handed to her. She flipped through the pages, the buzz of chatter wafting around her as she waited for the opening music.

A calm settled over her as the announcer's voice came through the speakers. The spotlight hit the stage. Kristy had seen the other designers' collections, both in the dressing rooms and at rehearsal. But nothing compared to seeing the creations strutted down the catwalk with the music blaring and a real audience applauding from the seats.

Kristy reached out to congratulate those closest to her as their models went by.

And then it was her turn.

She heard her name, felt the spotlight shift. And right then she didn't care that it was her second choice of a collection. She was part of this fabulous show, and it felt wonderful.

The spotlight hit the model, and Kristy jolted back in her seat, blinking in confusion. Lucinda was wearing the flirty waterfall dress. Kristy's swooping desert stripes glittered under the strong stage lights. The lacy crinoline bounced, showing off the sleek legs of the model.

Lucinda winked at Kristy as she passed by, but Kristy was too astounded to react. How had Zenia done it?

Next came the hot-air-balloon pants, with a pair of strappy black sandals, then the bikini and the sunset dress. By the time her roulette evening gown crossed the stage, Kristy recognized that the applause was strong and steady.

They liked her work.

They respected her talent.

She wanted to run backstage and wrap Zenia in her arms.

The contestant next to Kristy nudged her, and like the others before her, she rose and took a brief bow as the roulette-dress model headed back toward the curtain.

From his hard folding seat tucked away in a back corner, Jack watched the red evening gown disappear and shook his head in complete amazement.

She was great. She was better than great. And the collection, the collection was *them.* From the hot air balloon in the Grand Canyon to their night at the casino. Kristy had immortalized their whirlwind relationship in fashion.

He'd watched her face all through her part of the show. Her gaze had stayed on the models, and she'd smiled in response to comments from those around her, but he could tell she was still in shock.

God, she was gorgeous. And she was right—he hadn't given her nearly enough credit.

He patted the inside pocket of his suit, trying to figure out what he could possibly say that would convince her to take another chance on him. Things had started off badly between them, and he'd definitely let her down since. But if there was a speech on earth that would win her back, he was going to find it, and he was going to repeat it to her as many times as it took.

At the end of the show, the contest director took the stage. She gave a brief speech, congratulating the contestants and thanking the sponsors. She talked about the difficult choices of the judges and the enormous level of talent in the room.

Kristy only half listened.

Even when the drumroll sounded to signify the opening

of the judges' decision envelope, her attention was elsewhere. How had Zenia done it? *Why* had she done it? She had to find her and thank her.

"And now," the director's voice boomed, "the winner of this year's Matte Fashion Breakout Designer Contest is—"

She thought she saw Zenia at the side of the stage, and the rest of the words blurred in Kristy's ears.

"Kristy!" hissed the contestant next to her.

"Huh?"

"It's you!"

"What?" She glanced around and realized everyone was applauding madly and staring at her.

"Kristy Mahoney," the contest director repeated.

Kristy's entire body turned numb.

Her neighbor gave her a shove. "Get *up* there!"

Kristy forced herself to stand up on her shaky legs. She found the staircase and made her way to the stage, staring past the smiling director, past the curtain, even past Zenia.

And then she was at the microphone, and the director was shaking her hand. It was overwhelming, and she had no idea what to say.

And the applause was dwindling.

And she was supposed to start talking now.

Luckily, she couldn't see any of the audience members past the bright floodlights, or she probably would have passed out.

"Thank you," she managed, her voice quavering. "Thanks to the judges, to the sponsors, especially to Sierra Sanchez. To Cleveland Osland for believing in me. To Jack and Hunter Osland for their incredible support. And to Zenia Topaz." Kristy paused, gathering her emotions. "Zenia. I can't thank you enough for everything."

Kristy paused long enough that the applause began again. The models gathered around her, looking wonderful in her creations, congratulating her as the audience came to its feet. In her memory, she saw the waterfall, the hot air balloon, the casino and Jack. Jack was everywhere, in everything, and she desperately wanted to see him.

She needed to hear his voice, to feel his arms around her. She needed to taste him, to smell him, to hold him tight against her body long into the night. But mostly, she just needed him to be here, to breathe the same air as her, to tell her what he thought about the show, to tell her what he thought about the world.

Suddenly, she couldn't get off the stage fast enough.

She was going to call him.

No. She was going to fly back to L.A., or to New York, or to wherever he was at the moment. She'd beg him for another chance. The clothes didn't matter. The award didn't matter. All she wanted was Jack.

She made her way off the stage, smiling, automatically responding to people with what she hoped was logic.

She found Zenia and hugged her tight. "How did you do it?"

Zenia drew back from her. "I didn't. It was—"

"Do you have a cell phone?" Kristy interrupted.

"Sure." Zenia produced a phone.

Kristy flipped it open. "I need a plane ticket. I want to go back to New York. Now. Tonight."

Zenia glanced to a spot past Kristy's ear. "Why?"

Kristy looked down at the phone. "It's Jack. I need the number for the airline."

"What about Jack?"

"I love him. I'm in love with him. Oh, Zenia, I never thought I'd say this, but I don't care about the collection. I mean, I'm thrilled." She hugged Zenia again. "And I'm so grateful you brought it. But it doesn't matter. What's the damn phone number of the airline?"

"It wasn't me," said Zenia.

Kristy blinked at her.

"It was Jack."

"What was Jack?"

"Jack sent the collection from Vermont."

Kristy's heart stilled.

"About time I started to get a little credit," said Jack from behind her.

Kristy whirled around in astonishment.

He grinned at her, looking gorgeous and sexy and *here*. So here. He opened his arms, and she threw herself into them.

"How much did you hear?" she demanded.

"That you love me."

Kristy was embarrassed, but she wasn't about to take back the words now. "Eavesdropper," she accused.

"Hell, yeah. It's the only way I learn anything." He winked at Zenia. "Come on," he said to Kristy, taking her hand to lead her through the crowd.

"Where are we going?" Not that she cared. She glanced back to share a smile with Zenia.

"I want to show you something." Jack led her from the backstage area, down a small hallway and past a man in a security blazer.

"Where are you taking me?" she asked.

"Just wait," he answered, as they came out into a round, glassed-in room overlooking a rainswept garden and a group of lighted fountains.

"Hey," said Kristy. "This reminds me of Vegas."

"I know." Jack cracked a self-satisfied smile.

Then he led her to a painted, wrought-iron chair that sat next to the window. With the raindrops splattering on the glass and concrete, he motioned for her to sit down.

She perched on the edge of the chair and crossed her legs, staring into his dark eyes. She loved him so much.

He took a breath. "It occurs to me—" he said, reaching into his jacket pocket and coming down on one knee.

Before the significance of the position could register with Kristy, he revealed a turquoise jewelry box and opened it to expose a huge solitaire diamond ring. "—that I may not have done this right the first time."

Kristy's eyes went wide, first staring at the ring, and then staring at Jack.

"Will you marry me, Kristy? Or at least be kind enough not to divorce me?" He quirked an unexpected grin, leaning closer. "Because I think I figured out what's between us."

She felt her own mouth stretch into a smile. "Yeah? Well it's about time."

"As I recall, you were having the same problem."

"*I* already said it."

He cocked his head. "That was only ten minutes ago. I bought a ring and flew all the way from Manchester."

"Big whoop."

"Is that a yes?"

"Yeah," she told him. "That's a yes." She wrapped her arms around his neck and squeezed him tight. "Yours better be an 'I love you.'"

He rose to his feet, drawing her with him. "Mine's an 'I love you,'" he rumbled. "Mine's an 'I love you so much.'"

He tightened his arms around her waist, and she leaned her cheek against his chest, reveling in the feel of his strong, solid body. She had to blink away a tear.

"I loved your clothes," he rasped against her hair, cradling the back of her head with his palm. "I was so damn proud of you up there."

"You brought me my clothes." Part of her still couldn't believe it had happened.

"Damn straight," he said.

She pulled back to look at him. "But what changed your mind?"

"You changed my mind. Because you were right. I needed to stop playing it safe."

"Damn straight," she said back.

He grinned and placed a quick kiss on her lips. "Once I trusted your instincts, I started trusting my own."

"And?"

"And my instincts brought me right here, to you."

Then he kissed her again, while thunder rumbled in the distance. Raindrops clattered furiously against the glass.

He broke the kiss. "Can we please get this ring on your finger?"

She nodded and held out her hand.

He slipped the ring over her knuckle, anchoring the band in place. "I do love you, Kristy Mahoney."

She held her hand to the light, gazing at the twinkling diamond, joy filling her heart. "I think it's Kristy Osland now."

"Now." He kissed her knuckle above the stone. "And forever."

* * * * *

Don't miss Sinclair and Hunter's story
BEAUTY AND THE BILLIONAIRE
coming in February 2008!

SPECIAL EDITION®

Life, Love and Family

*These contemporary romances will strike a chord
with you as heroines juggle life
and relationships on their way to true love.*

New York Times *bestselling author Linda Lael Miller
brings you a BRAND-NEW contemporary story
featuring her fan-favorite McKettrick family.*

Meg McKettrick is surprised to be reunited with her
high school flame, Brad O'Ballivan. After enjoying a
career as a country-and-western singer, Brad aches for
a home and family...and seeing Meg again makes him
realize he still loves her. But their pride manages to
interfere with love...until an unexpected matchmaker
gets involved.

Turn the page for a sneak preview of
THE McKETTRICK WAY *by Linda Lael Miller*
On sale November 20, wherever books are sold.

Brad shoved the truck into gear and drove to the bottom of the hill, where the road forked. Turn left, and he'd be home in five minutes. Turn right, and he was headed for Indian Rock.

He had no damn business going to Indian Rock.

He had nothing to say to Meg McKettrick, and if he never set eyes on the woman again, it would be two weeks too soon.

He turned right.

He couldn't have said why.

He just drove straight to the Dixie Dog Drive-In.

Back in the day, he and Meg used to meet at the Dixie Dog, by tacit agreement, when either of them had been away. It had been some kind of universe thing, purely intuitive.

Passing familiar landmarks, Brad told himself he ought to turn around. The old days were gone. Things had ended badly between him and Meg anyhow, and she wasn't going to be at the Dixie Dog.

He kept driving.

He rounded a bend, and there was the Dixie Dog. Its big neon sign, a giant hot dog, was all lit up and going through its corny sequence—first it was covered in red squiggles of light, meant to suggest ketchup, and then yellow, for mustard.

Brad pulled into one of the slots next to a speaker, rolled down the truck window and ordered.

A girl roller-skated out with the order about five minutes later.

When she wheeled up to the driver's window, smiling, her eyes went wide with recognition, and she dropped the tray with a clatter.

Silently Brad swore. Damn if he hadn't forgotten he was a famous country singer.

The girl, a skinny thing wearing too much eye makeup, immediately started to cry. "I'm sorry!" she sobbed, squatting to gather up the mess.

"It's okay," Brad answered quietly, leaning to look down at her, catching a glimpse of her plastic name tag. "It's okay, Mandy. No harm done."

"I'll get you another dog and a shake right away, Mr. O'Ballivan!"

"Mandy?"

She stared up at him pitifully, sniffling. Thanks to the copious tears, most of the goop on her eyes had slid south. "Yes?"

"When you go back inside, could you not mention seeing me?"

"But you're Brad O'Ballivan!"

"Yeah," he answered, suppressing a sigh. "I know."

She rolled a little closer. "You wouldn't happen to have a picture you could autograph for me, would you?"

"Not with me," Brad answered.

"You could sign this napkin, though," Mandy said. "It's only got a little chocolate on the corner."

Brad took the paper napkin and her order pen, and scrawled his name. Handed both items back through the window.

She turned and whizzed back toward the side entrance to the Dixie Dog.

Brad waited, marveling that he hadn't considered incidents like this one before he'd decided to come back home. In retrospect, it seemed shortsighted, to say the least, but the truth was, he'd expected to be—Brad O'Ballivan.

Presently Mandy skated back out again, and this time she managed to hold on to the tray.

"I didn't tell a soul!" she whispered. "But Heather and Darlene *both* asked me why my mascara was all smeared." Efficiently she hooked the tray onto the bottom edge of the window.

Brad extended payment, but Mandy shook her head.

"The boss said it's on the house, since I dumped your first order on the ground."

He smiled. "Okay, then. Thanks."

Mandy retreated, and Brad was just reaching for the food when a bright red Blazer whipped into the space beside his. The driver's door sprang open, crashing into the metal speaker, and somebody got out in a hurry.

Something quickened inside Brad.

And in the next moment Meg McKettrick was standing practically on his running board, her blue eyes blazing.

Brad grinned. "I guess you're not over me after all," he said.

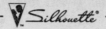

SPECIAL EDITION™

**brings you a heartwarming
new McKettrick's story from**

NEW YORK TIMES BESTSELLING AUTHOR

LINDA LAEL MILLER

THE McKETTRICK
Way

Meg McKettrick is surprised to be reunited
with her high school flame, Brad O'Ballivan,
who has returned home to his family's
neighboring ranch. After seeing Meg again,
Brad realizes he still loves her. But the pride
of both manage to interfere with love...until
an unexpected matchmaker gets involved.

—— McKettrick Women ——

Available December wherever you buy books.

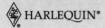

EVERLASTING LOVE™

Every great love has a story to tell™

Every Christmas gift Will and Dinah
exchange is a symbol of their love.
The tradition began on their very first
date and continues through every holiday
season—whether they're together or apart—
until tragedy strikes. And then only an
unexpected gift can make things right.

Look for

Christmas Presents and Past

by
Janice Kay Johnson

Available December wherever you buy books.

COMING NEXT MONTH

#1837 THE EXECUTIVE'S SURPRISE BABY—
Catherine Mann
The Garrisons
The news of his impending fatherhood was shocking…
discovering the mother of his baby didn't want to marry him—
unbelievable.

#1838 SPENCER'S FORBIDDEN PASSION—
Brenda Jackson
A Westmoreland bachelor got more than he bargained for when
he turned his hostile takeover bid into a marriage-of-convenience
offer.

#1839 RICH MAN'S VENGEFUL SEDUCTION—
Laura Wright
No Ring Required
He had one goal: seduce the woman who left him years ago and
leave her cold. Could he carry out his plan after a night together
ignites old passions?

#1840 MARRIED OR NOT?—Annette Broadrick
The last person she needed or wanted to see was her
ex-husband…until she discovered they could still be man and
wife.

#1841 HIS STYLE OF SEDUCTION—Roxanne St. Claire
She was charged with giving this millionaire a makeover. But she
was the one in for a big change...in the bedroom.

#1842 THE MAGNATE'S MARRIAGE DEMAND—
Robyn Grady
A wealthy tycoon demanded the woman pregnant with the heir
to his family dynasty marry him. But their passionate union was
anything but all business.